Sue's Vision

Andrew D. Carlson

This is a work of fiction. Names, characters, places and incidents either are the product of the author's imagination or are used fictitiously, and any resemblance to actual persons, living or dead, business establishments, events, or locales is entirely coincidental.

SUE'S VISION

ISBN: 0615590497
ISBN-13: 978-0-615-59049-3

Dedication

To David

Rest in Peace

Cast of Characters

<u>Enterprise, Kansas</u>

Suzanne "Sue" Cook (clone) – cook, Smokey Hill Café

Violet (clone) – 7 y/o

Kati (clone) – 6 y/o

David Hudson – retired

Zachary (clone) – 12 y/o

Tyler (clone) – 8 y/o

Susan Roberts – archivist, DDE Presidential Library

Karen – 7 y/o

Petunia Clark – retired

<u>Washington, D.C.</u>

Ted Stevens – Director, DHS

<u>Tempe, Arizona</u>

Martha Ross (clone) – barista, Cupz

Patsy Sharp (clone) – student & barista, Cupz

Richard Dvorak – student, Arizona State University

<u>Burbank, California</u>

Donald Jackson (clone) – clerk, DHS

Denise Jackson – analyst, DHS

Brandy (clone) – 13 y/o

Juliana Huffington – analyst, DHS

<u>Spring Green, Wisconsin</u>

Larry Stone (clone) – farmhand

Janet Jones (clone) – shop worker, Arena Cheese, Inc.

Mary MacDonald – retired

<u>Manhattan, Kansas</u>

Jim Bailey, Ph.D. – Director, Manhattan Laboratory Services

Sarah Deming – analyst, MLS

Cindy Gordon – analyst, MLS

Bruno Jones, Ph.D. – analyst, MLS

As best as can be determined, the world is now warmer than it has been at any point in the last two millennia, and, if current trends continue, by the end of the century it will likely be hotter than at any point in the last two million years.

In the same way that global warming has gradually ceased to be merely a theory, so, too, its impacts are no longer just hypothetical.

It may seem impossible to imagine that a technologically advanced society could choose, in essence, to destroy itself, but that is what we are now in the process of doing.

Elizabeth Kolbert, Annals of Science, "The Climate of Man - I," *The New Yorker*, April 25, 2005, p. 56.

Chapter 1 - Scribbles

Sue returned from work in the afternoon. She rode her bicycle down the road, turned into the driveway and parked in David's garage. Learning to ride a bike was one of the first things she did when she relocated to Kansas. She didn't want to rely on others for transportation; she wanted the freedom to get herself where she wanted to go.

As usual, she smelled like the Smokey Hill Café. Of the breakfast and lunch crowd at the café, Sue was the favorite short-order cook. She greeted customers through the pick-up window when they sat at the counter, and she'd even walk through the café, when time allowed, chatting with the people of Enterprise. And Sue was a good cook. She had learned her craft well. Smelling like the café at the end of each day was a badge of pride for Sue. Her job was a symbol of her independence.

She walked through the door from the garage to the backyard and greeted David.

"Welcome home, Sue," he replied with a smile.

"Come out here and relax while the sun is still shining." He pulled a chair away from the patio table and offered it to her. He added, "I'm sorry you had to work today."

"It's okay," she replied cheerfully and sat in the chair. "I didn't mind covering the kitchen while the others did the catering for the Larson reunion. It was actually kinda fun. I haven't worked a Sunday in a long time. It was more relaxed than on a weekday. What did I miss here?"

"The carpenter came today and installed the cabinets in your kitchen. Do you want to go see them?"

"Yeah, let's go!" Sue sprang to her feet. They walked past the trailer that served as Sue's temporary housing and toward the new house at the far end of David's lot.

On the outside, the new house was finished. It was a white, two-story traditional house. It blended in well with the rest of the neighborhood. The inside still needed a bit more work, but it was nearly finished.

As David and Sue walked in the front door, he told her, "You'll be moving in soon."

"I can't wait! I'll have my own house with lots of space and a new kitchen!"

"How do the cabinets look?" David inquired.

"Great! I love them!" she said, beaming with happiness. She could hardly contain her excitement. "When do the counters arrive? And when do the stove and refrigerator and dishwasher arrive? And when will the bathrooms be done?"

"They kitchen stuff will be here this week, maybe as early as tomorrow or Tuesday. The installers are supposed to call. The bathrooms will be the last to be done. I hope it's no more than two weeks until you move in."

"Then we can move that trailer out of your yard. And put in a pool!"

"A pool?" David asked. "Who said anything about a pool?"

"Well, I think it's a great idea. The kids need a pool. I'll ask Ted if he'll pay for a pool. He will."

"No he won't. At least I don't think he will. Do you think he will? Really?"

"He likes me, David," Sue replied. "He will."

She stood in her soon-to-be-finished kitchen and smiled. She was excited to be so close to moving into the new house and, more importantly, out of the temporary one. She gave one final look around and then said to David, "C'mon, let's go see the kids."

She and David exited the house, locked the door and headed back toward the children's game in the yard. Kati and Violet were playing in the yard with Tyler and Zachary.

Although the four young clones weren't related when they "arrived" from the alien "goo" the previous September, and even though Zachary and Tyler lived with David while Kati and Violet lived with Sue, the kids thought of themselves as brothers and sisters. They went through the same experiences together while "growing up" over the last seven months, which bonded them together like siblings. And they played together like they were.

The game that day was touch football; boys versus girls. It shouldn't have been a fair game since Zachary was almost twice as old as the girls and as big as any other twelve year old going on thirteen. And Tyler was taller and more solid than most other eight year old boys. But they were playing Kati. Even though she was only six, she played like she was much older. Kati was a shy little girl when she first arrived, but after moving to Kansas, with Sue as her mother, she became outgoing and competitive. She didn't let the boys go easy on her just because she was a girl. Violet, on the other hand, was more feminine than Kati. She was, after all, almost eight, as she often reminded her sister. But she still played the games. She'd rush the quarterback, as long as she didn't fall or get pushed down and get too dirty.

"Time out! Mom coming through the field! Time out!" Sue announced. When she reached the kids, she asked, "Can I have five minutes to hear what happened today?"

"The boys woke us up this morning," Violet informed her mother. "They decided our trailer needed to be part of their army game."

"Yeah," Kati chimed in, "they were loud and making their dumb shooting noises."

"Boys!" David scolded them with his hands on his hips. "I told you not to play near their house in the morning. You know better."

Sue raised her hand at David to stop him, and then calmly looked at her daughters. "Girls, what time did they wake you up?"

"Um... it was like... nine o'clock," Kati cautiously replied.

"Maybe it was closer to nine-thirty," Violet sheepishly volunteered.

"I see," Sue flatly replied. "You're complaining about being woken up at nine-thirty?" she confirmed. The girls hung their heads and shuffled their feet. Turning to Tyler and Zachary, Sue smiled and reassured them, "Boys, you are not in trouble. If the girls are still in bed at nine o'clock, you can play outside. Besides, we'll be in the new house soon, so you'll have the whole yard to play in without waking the girls."

When she finished talking, Sue noticed Karen run around David's garage and into the yard. "Karen," she called out, "my little sister, how are you today?"

"Good, Sue! How was work today?" Karen asked when she came up to the others in the middle of the yard.

"Splendid. Are you just now coming over to play?" she asked.

"No, I was here this morning. I just had to go back home to help my mom for a little bit."

Karen was the daughter of Susan Roberts; the original Sue. It was Susan who touched the alien substance which made an exact copy of her. Sue, the clone, spent many days at Susan's house with Karen while waiting to be relocated by DHS. Karen taught Sue how to read, and introduced her to cartoons on the TV. They laughed and played together as sisters. Sue had a special place in her heart for Karen.

"What does everyone want for dinner tonight?" David asked. "I need to call Susan and Petunia to coordinate."

"I'll do it," Sue offered.

"No. You won't," David replied. "You worked all day. Please sit and relax. I can cook. Really, I can."

"Hamburgers!" the boys requested.

"And corn on the cob!" Kati added.

"Kati, it's barely April. No corn on the cob yet," Karen told her. "You have to wait until summer."

"I keep forgetting. I gotta remember that corn doesn't grow all year here."

"We can get frozen corn off the cob," David

suggested. It's almost as good. What about potato salad?" he asked the kids.

"Yeah, but not that German kind that Mrs. Clark brings," Violet said. "No offense, but it's yucky. I like the normal kind."

"Okay, I'll make the arrangements."

"Can we eat outside?" Tyler asked.

"Dude! It's gonna be dark soon and it'll be too cold," Zachary responded with a punch to his brother's arm.

"Ow! Cut it out, man!" Tyler whined.

"Okay, okay. You all go finish the game," Sue ordered. "I'm going to change my clothes and relax," she called out as she walked to her temporary home. The kids resumed playing football and David went inside his house to call their neighbors and make dinner plans.

After a few minutes, Sue emerged from her trailer wearing a clean set of clothes and carrying sunscreen and her laptop. She sprayed her face and arms with the sunscreen and sat at the patio table to enjoy a few minutes of sun. She booted up her laptop, read the new email messages, and deleted the old messages and spam from her account. She also took a few minutes to send an email to Ted Stevens, making her case for a new swimming pool in the yard.

David came out through the screen door, handed Sue a glass of iced tea, and sat with her at the table. Sue smiled at David and thanked him for the drink. He returned the smile and the two sat in pleasant silence watching the kids play in the yard.

David Hudson was a retired military officer. He had served in various high-profile, "special" assignments and was now enjoying retirement at his relatively young age of forty-six.

When Ted Stevens had first approached him in November and asked him to look after Sue and the young clones who were relocating to Enterprise, David was reluctant. He had lived his life as a free man. He had no wife or children. He didn't think he wanted to be tied down.

But then he gave the idea more thought. He knew who Sue was from the previous September when she first arrived. He helped keep an eye on her before DHS arranged to pick her up. He was also there when Sue escaped from the base to deliver her message to her "family" in Enterprise. He knew how much trouble she could be. But he also knew how determined she was to learn and discover new things. Sue intrigued him. Ted told him the kids would be equally enthusiastic to learn and grow. And David loved a challenge, so he agreed to Ted's proposal.

After being with Sue for a few months, David became the yin to Sue's yang. He balanced Sue's excitement with tranquility. He provided Sue with the experience that she lacked. And he kept her grounded when she had the impulse to fly off and discover new things. He agreed to the assignment from Ted, but it became much more than just a duty to him. It became his new life.

From around the corner of the house, their neighbors, Petunia and Susan arrived. Sue got up to greet them, and then offered each a chair around the table.

Susan Roberts and Suzanne Cook, *a.k.a.* Sue, sat next to each other as they shared news and gossip. Although they told everyone in Enterprise they were cousins, they looked like identical twins--which they were. Both were tall, slim, and fit. Susan continued to wear her sandy brown hair short; the trick David suggested to tell her apart from her clone when the other Sue arrived. Sue kept her hair long, tied in a ponytail. Susan wore slacks, skirts and dresses, while Sue preferred jeans and t-shirts. Susan wore a little eye shadow and lipstick while Sue didn't wear any. Makeup didn't last long in the kitchen of the Smokey Hill café.

"How was the café today, Sue?" Susan asked.

"Not bad. It was slower than usual. I actually enjoyed it. But I don't want to work weekends all the time, only when I have to, you know, to help the restaurant when needed."

"You're a good person Sue. They're lucky to have you at the Smokey Hill," Susan told her. "I'm glad I don't get asked to work at the museum on the weekends."

"From what I hear around town, you're the most popular cook at the café, Sue," Petunia told her. "Weren't you even offered the cashier position?"

"Yes, but I didn't want to do that," Sue replied. "I want to cook."

"And I'm sure the customers prefer you cooking. They love your recipes," Susan told her.

"Thanks," Sue proudly responded.

"David," Petunia observed, "you seemed to have survived by yourself today with all the children. I didn't hear you holler from across the street, so I guess all went well."

"Or maybe they tied you up so you couldn't yell," Susan jokingly suggested.

"I had a great day with the kids," David replied, smiling. He ran his fingers through his graying crew-cut hair and leaned back in his chair. He wore a plain faded t-shirt, ragged cargo shorts, old sneakers, and his Swiss army watch. The constant smile that he now wore on his face took five years off his hardened, gruff, military appearance. He had a new vitality now that Zachary and Tyler were officially part of his life. And he enjoyed having Sue and her girls around too. "They didn't gang up on me, which I thought they all would," he replied to Petunia and Susan. "The boys protected me from the girls," he added, "which is unusual because they always try to tackle me and hold me down. I guess they felt a duty to protect dear old dad."

Petunia looked to the game in the yard and commented, "I'm always amazed how well they all play with each other. Five kids from different beginnings are now the best of friends."

"We're lucky," Sue replied.

"Yes we are," Susan added.

The sun dropped below tree level. David called to the kids to go inside and clean up. He rose and said, "You ladies can stay out here in the dark or you can come inside. It's your choice." He flashed them a grin.

The women stood and followed David inside his house. On her way, Sue told Kati and Violet to change into jeans for dinner, not shorts. Susan handed Karen a bag containing the change of clothes she brought over.

The adults took seats at the kitchen table and resumed their conversation. "Are the girls getting excited about moving into the new house?" Susan asked Sue.

"I think so. But they're not nearly as excited as I am. I can't wait to get in that house."

"You have a room for Karen too, correct?" Petunia asked Sue. "She'll want to stay there every day

I think."

"The girls' room is big enough for all three," Sue replied. "I just hope the walls are thick enough to keep the sound down."

"They do tend to get a little loud, don't they?" David asked.

"Yeah, they do," Zachary called out from around the corner.

"Yeah! They're really loud!" Tyler added.

"So are you two sometimes," David called back.

"They all are sometimes," Susan commented, "but I'm glad they have each other to play with."

"Shall I start cooking?" David asked.

The others agreed.

David started preparing dinner, moving back and forth between the kitchen and the grill outside on his patio. The girls returned from their trailer and cut through the kitchen to the front room to see what the boys were doing. The ladies continued talking at the table.

When dinner was served, the herd of children rumbled into the kitchen and took seats at a card table that David set up. David served them first to quiet the chaos. He also couldn't wait for Sue's house to be finished so they could use her kitchen which was substantially larger.

After eating, Susan and Petunia offered to help David clean the dishes and the kitchen. Sue offered too, but was rejected by all three.

Instead of cleaning, Sue asked the kids if they wanted to play a game. She told them she had a fun new game that she learned at the Café. "It's a story game. You make up stories about people and change the words so they're funnier than the original story."

"Oh, Mad Libs," David replied.

"Huh?" Sue replied. The kids mirrored her look of confusion.

"Yeah, Mad Libs," Susan added. "You have a story and change nouns and verbs and adjectives to make a funnier story. We played that game all the time when we were kids, especially on road trips."

"I didn't know it was called that, but yeah… I guess that's the game," Sue responded. Turning to the kids, she continued, "Let's make a story about David."

"Yeah!" Tyler replied. "Let's make it really funny."

"Okay, we have to write the boring story first." Sue began, "One day…"

"Dad was building something in his garage when he hit his thumb with his hammer," Zachary suggested.

"Yeah! And he said a really bad word," Tyler added. He laughed with his brother.

The girls laughed too.

"That's funny boys. But let's start with a boring story first, then we can change it so he hits his thumb and says bad words. Can you go get me a piece of paper and pencil?" she asked Zachary.

While Zachary ran to his dad's office, Sue continued, "Okay, let's start with… One day, David was working in the garage when his sons came in. He said to the boys 'I'm building a…' What should he build?" she asked.

"Here you go," Zachary said when he returned, handing Sue the paper and pencil.

"Okay, let's write this down." As Sue wrote, she repeated the story, "One day, David was working in the garage--"

"Hey!" Karen interrupted. "What are you writing? That's not the story. You're scribbling."

"No she's not," Tyler said.

"Yeah," Kati replied, defending her mother. "It says 'One day, David was working'--"

"No, it doesn't," Karen insisted.

"Sure it does," Violet replied. Zachary nodded in agreement.

"That's just a bunch of scribbles," Karen protested.

David walked over to the table to mediate. He looked at the paper and stopped. He stood silent for a few moments, and then quietly said to Sue, "It looks like a bunch of scribbles. Those aren't words."

"Yes, they are," Sue replied. "It says--"

"I know what you think it says, but that's not what you wrote," he told her.

Sue looked at him confused. "What do you mean?"

David looked at the boys, Kati and Violet. "Can you read this?"

"Yeah," they each replied.

"Can you, Karen?" Sue asked.

"No," Karen answered.

David picked up the paper, turned it over and held it up to the light for Sue to see the writing backwards. "Can you read it now?" he asked.

"No, I can't. It looks like scribbles now." Sue frowned at the paper David was holding, trying to understand. "What does that mean?"

"It means that you and the kids can read and write a new language."

Chapter 2 - A Pool

"A pool? How much does she think she needs?" Ted asked out loud as he read Sue's email on his cell phone. He glanced up at the road and quickly answered his own question, "What am I saying? She's Sue! She needs whatever she asks for."

What had started as a simple assignment from DHS to investigate a gel-like substance, later turned into a life-changing event for everyone involved. Throughout the months he was ordered to "recover the aliens" that had arrived on the planet and "contain them" on the decommissioned air force base, he got to know the clones personally. He began to see their personalities emerge and learn their preferences and desires. He especially came to like and respect Sue, the first of the eleven people cloned from the substance that appeared on Earth. Ted admired her persistence and playful intensity. It was Sue's tenacity to learn and desire to be free that ultimately led him to defy his superiors and release the clones. Ted considered the clones his friends and committed himself to enhancing their lives, even if it meant having to procure a pool for Sue.

As he drove down I-70 to Enterprise, Kansas, Ted dialed his colleague, Jim Bailey, at Manhattan Laboratory Services, a few miles east of where he was going.

"Jim! It's Ted. How are you? ... Good. That's good to hear. Listen, I've got to give the committee an update in a couple weeks. I need to tell them about the experiments you all are doing, as well as what our friends are up to. When can I drop by and get a de-briefing from you? ... Can you do it as early as tomorrow? ... Great! I'll be there at eight. See you then. ... Have a good day, Jim."

Ted put his phone back in the pocket of his Hawaiian shirt, leaned back in his seat and enjoyed the drive. Since releasing the clones, Ted had a new look on life and it showed. His new, personally-approved work attire was khaki pants and Hawaiian shirts. If he went to Arizona or California, he authorized shorts instead of pants. Only if he had a meeting with the Committee in Washington was he forced to put on his "monkey suit." When away from Washington, he continually wore a smile and walked with an air of confidence. He knew he made the right decision. He knew the clones were not alien beings, and he was sure they would not take over the world. He enjoyed proving that to the department every day.

In November, his assignment was modified by DHS to "continually assess the threat posed by the alien new people." He had a substantial budget to keep things quiet and a jet at his disposal to travel between the various cities where the former base residents had been relocated.

As he drove, he thought to himself that he could have been doing a lot of things for the department much less enjoyable than traveling all over the country visiting his friends.

Chapter 3 - You're the Boss

A little before 3:00 in the afternoon, a convertible sports car pulled into David's driveway. A man in khakis and a Hawaiian shirt got out and walked to the house.

David came out of his garage and shook hands with the man. "Hi Ted."

"Thanks for meeting me, David."

"No problem."

"Can we go see the new house?" Ted asked.

"Sure."

They walked to the house in the back of the yard. David unlocked the door and the two men walked in. "This is nice," said Ted. "What's left? It looks like the kitchen is close to complete. Sue must be drooling. I bet she can't wait to move in."

"She's excited," David told Ted. "I have to give her an update every day after she comes home from work. The kitchen should be finished this week, bathrooms and furniture next week. Then it's done."

After taking a quick tour upstairs, they left the

house and stood in the front yard. "What brought you out here today?" David inquired. "What can I do for you?"

"I wanted to talk with you about Sue and the kids. I want to know if you have detected anything. Have you seen anything unusual... something I should be concerned about?"

"The kids all play well with each other," David said. "No sudden changes or crazy outbursts or anything like that, unless Zachary beats up on Tyler. But that's just boys being boys. The girls are perfect. They're all the right height and weight and all that stuff. And Sue... well, she's Sue. She knows what she wants and gets it. She's always happy to learn and try new things. And she loves to help. She's never done anything..." He paused.

Sensing David's hesitation, Ted said, "You're holding something back. What is it?"

"It's nothing," David reassured Ted, waving his hand. But then he added, "Or... at least I think it's nothing."

"David," Ted sternly replied, "Give." He folded his arms and faced David. "What's going on? What have you seen?"

"Sue and the kids were playing a game. They were writing down words to make funny sentences. But they weren't writing in English."

"What language? Has Sue learned Spanish already?" Ted laughed.

"It wasn't anything I've ever seen," David replied plainly, not laughing with Ted. "It looked like scribbling on the paper. I asked the kids if they could read what Sue was writing. They said they could. But Karen couldn't. You think they were messing with me?"

"A new language?" Ted asked. The smile faded from his face. "And neither you nor Karen could read it?"

"Yeah. And neither could Susan or Petunia. So I tried something; I turned the paper over and held it up so the writing was backwards. Sue couldn't read it then."

"A new language that only she and the other clones can read… This is new," he said. He thought to himself for a few moments, and then asked David, "Why'd you hold back?"

"I wasn't sure if it was real," David replied. "I wasn't sure they weren't playing a joke on me. I don't want to make a big deal out of it."

"Fair enough," Ted said, letting the subject drop for now. "So, what's for dinner?"

"I don't know. I haven't really thought about it. I usually leave that up to Sue. I'm sure the kids will have suggestions, but Sue will override them and come up with something else."

"When does Sue get home?" Ted asked.

"Soon," David replied, looking at his watch. "She usually gets home a few minutes after the kids. And they'll be home any second."

Right on cue, the bus stopped at the intersection down the road. Three girls and two boys ran around the front of the bus and didn't stop running until they reached the backyard. They dropped their backpacks and Karen grabbed the football. Zachary and Violet managed to greet Ted with a quick, "Hi Ted!" The younger kids were too preoccupied to notice the visitor standing in the yard.

"This is what it's like every day," David told

Ted. "At least now they can play outside instead of being cooped up inside for the winter. They'll play until it gets dark."

"Lots of energy, eh?"

"Lots."

Just as David predicted, by the time the football game started, Sue rode her bike down the street, onto the driveway and into David's garage. She came around the house with a huge smile on her face. "Ted!"

"Hello, Sue. How are you?"

"Great!" she said, giving Ted a big hug. "What are you doing here?"

"Well, you see, regulations require I survey the backyard personally before I authorize installing a pool," Ted replied sarcastically with a wink.

"A pool? We're getting a pool?" Kati screamed after overhearing Ted's comment. "Cool!"

"Oh, crap," Ted said, hitting his forehead with the palm of his hand.

"You should know, Ted," Sue advised, "don't promise what you don't want to deliver."

"Me and my big mouth," Ted said. "Me and my big mouth."

"Are you staying for dinner, Ted?" Sue asked. "David, did you call Susan and Petunia? We should have something good. What sounds good?"

You're the boss," Ted replied.

"Ditto," added David.

"Fine, roasted chicken and potatoes it is. I'll call Susan. Let me change and we can sit and relax. How's that sound?"

"You're the boss."

"Ditto."

Sue went into her temporary home and started

changing. As they stood in the yard, the two men heard a loud thud from inside the trailer. "Ow!" was the response from Sue, followed by banging against a wall. "Two more weeks and I'm out of this trailer and into my big house!" Sue yelled with both frustration and anticipation. Ted and David only grinned at each other, not saying a word that she might hear. Shortly after, Sue calmly emerged from the trailer as if nothing happened inside. She wore dressy shorts and a print shirt for her guest. She smiled when she joined David and Ted.

David asked, "Can I get you both something to drink?"

"Iced Tea for me, please," Sue requested.

"Got a beer?" asked Ted.

"Coming right up," David replied. He went into the house to get the drinks.

Sue and Ted walked to the patio and sat down at the table. "You look good, Ted. Still wearing the fancy Hawaiian shirts?"

"Yep, they're better than wearing a suit. You look good too," he offered with a smile. "How are things at the café? Are you still everyone's favorite cook?"

"I think so. We have lots of loyal customers. Why are you here?"

Ted snapped his head back in surprise, stunned at her boldness. She didn't glare at him. Rather, she sat up tall and looked at him confidently. She knew there was a reason he was at her home. He answered, "I'm just checking in. Does that surprise you?"

"No. But I always have to ask," she replied assertively. "There might be another reason."

"You're smart, Sue. You are smart."

"So?" she asked, expecting another reason.
"I'm just checking in," Ted calmly replied.

Chapter 4 - Arizona

Martha took the opportunity of a cool day--a cool day for Tempe, Arizona--to sit on the balcony of her apartment. The air outside was dry and eighty-five degrees: perfect weather. She diligently applied her sunscreen, pulled a shot of espresso, and then took it outside along with her computer.

She launched her email program and scanned for new messages. Nothing important caught her attention, so she composed a new message to her best friend:

Dear Sue,

How are things with you and the kids? The weather must be getting warmer in Kansas. You don't have any snow any more, do you? As always, it is beautiful here in Arizona.

Nothing new has happened here since we last emailed each other. I'm still working the opening shift at Cupz. I love seeing all those college students each morning. I love to see them excited for another day of learning, even though most of them are half asleep. They remind me of you: always wanting to learn.

Speaking of learning, Patsy continues to study hard. She is doing really well. She is so smart to learn so much as fast as she has. I think she'll be ready to take the GED test soon, which is pretty amazing. She's had to learn a lot. I hope she does well on the test so she can go to college next year. Between me working at Cupz in the morning and her studying all day and into the night, I hardly ever see her, except on the weekends for a little bit and at dinner. I thought she'd be too busy to keep coming back to the apartment to have dinner with me every night, but she isn't. She always comes back for dinner. I like it that we can have an hour or so together. I know that I'm not alone here.

Oh, I almost forgot. Patsy has a study buddy. His name is Richard. I met him a couple times. He seems really nice. And Patsy seems to like him too. I think he's a year or two older than Patsy, but they seem to get along together well.

That's all from AZ. I hope all is well in KS!

Your friend, Martha

Martha smiled. She reflected on her short life so far and thought about all that had happened since September. She appeared from out of nowhere in Rockford, Illinois, after her other person touched the alien substance. The police put her in jail to wait until Mr. Stevens picked her up and took her to the base in California. It was on the base where she met Sue and Donald and the boys; the other clones, they later found out. Then the second group of clones was brought to the base, including Patsy. She remembered how they all learned together. And she learned to make coffee.

A warm feeling rose inside her as she sat on the balcony. Coffee was her elixir of life. And brewing it was her passion. And since Ted had released the clones in November to live as they wanted, coffee was the symbol of her freedom.

She relaxed in her chair as the sun began to set. The color of her face--darkened slightly by the Arizona sun, despite the constant use of sunscreen--along with the smile she always wore made her look younger than when she first arrived. Of course she had only appeared six months ago, but then she looked to be around sixty--the age of the person from whom she was cloned. Customers at Cupz didn't think she was much older than fifty.

A few minutes later, Patsy arrived at the apartment and called out to Martha. She followed Martha's voice and joined her on the balcony. "Hey roomie, how was your day?"

"Wonderful. And yours?" Martha asked.

"Not bad, you know, the usual," Patsy replied. "I studied all day. Not much excitement in that, is there?"

"Except that it will get you a degree soon."

"Yes it will," Patsy replied with a big grin. "Yes it will." She took a seat in the other chair. Patsy's long legs didn't leave a lot of room on their small balcony, but she and Martha had the chairs carefully arranged to maximize the space. Patsy looked over at Martha through her sunglasses and asked, "How was work today, the usual for you, too?"

"Yep, the usual for me, too," Martha replied

with a smile. "We had solid business all morning. Not much time to talk with anyone. But I had a few moments before the after-lunch crowd came in for their caffeine boost."

"I hope tonight is calm," Patsy said. "I'd like to have a little bit of time to talk to Richard. Usually I can break away for 15 minutes, but not if we're slammed."

"I hope you don't mind," Martha said cautiously, "but I mentioned Richard to Sue in an email that I just sent her. I hope that's okay."

"Sure," Patsy replied.

"Since you and Richard seem to be spending more time studying together, I thought that it would be okay to tell Sue about him," Martha said, still looking for approval.

"Yeah, no problem," Patsy said with a smile. "That's cool. He and I are getting more serious, I think. We're starting to talk about our personal lives more." She paused, took off her sunglasses and looked at Martha before continuing, "I'm actually thinking about telling him where I came from."

"Really?" Martha asked, shocked at the idea. "What do you think he'll say? He'll probably think you're crazy."

"Maybe," Patsy replied calmly. "But if we're going to be serious, he's going to have to find out. Maybe not now, but sometime soon he'll have to find out."

Martha looked nervously at Patsy. She agreed with her that if Patsy and Richard were going to be dating he would have to find out at some time in the future, but yet, she wasn't sure how he'd react to knowing Patsy was a clone.

A ping sounded from Martha's computer,

telling her she had received an email message. Martha looked at her email account. "It's a response from Sue," she told her roommate. "Should I read it?"

"Yeah, go ahead," Patsy replied.

"Happy Day, Martha," she began reading. "Tell me about Patsy's study friend. Are they boyfriend and girlfriend, or just friends? Is he nice? What does he look like? Tell me more."

Martha turned to Patsy, raised her eyebrows, and silently asked if it was okay to give Sue more details.

"Go ahead. You know Sue; she won't let it go until you tell her everything," Patsy replied.

You're right," Martha said. "I'll tell her all I know." She turned her head back to her computer and continued reading Sue's email, "The kitchen cabinets were installed at my new house today. David says we have two weeks until the girls and I can move in. I can hardly wait! Your friend always, Sue."

"When you reply," Patsy told Martha, "say 'Hi' from me and tell her that I'm glad that she'll be in her new house soon, okay? Now, let's make dinner."

Chapter 5 - Way to go!

The intercom buzzed. Denise walked from the kitchen to answer it, "Juliana?"

"Yeah, it's me."

"C'mon up. The door's open."

A few moments later, there was a knock at the door and Juliana entered. Denise met her at the door and they hugged.

The two women first met when they were assigned to work as staff members at the base. Ted Stevens had hand-picked them from within the department. Denise was chosen because of her security clearance and her past experience as a youth camp director. Juliana was selected for her psychology degree and training within the department administering behavior and profile testing. During the two months spent monitoring and helping the "residents" at the base, the two women became best friends.

When the clones were released, Denise returned to her old position within DHS in Los Angeles. But she left the base with more than she came with. She left with Donald, a clone, and married him a month later. She also left with Brandy, one of the five young clones. She and Donald adopted Brandy as their daughter. The time spent at the base teaching all of the clones and helping them discover themselves brought out the motherly instinct in Denise. She was happy to start a new life with her family.

When released from duty, Juliana decided she wanted to join her new friend and her new friend's family. She had no husband, nor even a boyfriend, so moving to a new city was not a big deal. Ted willingly made the arrangements to reassign and relocate her to L.A.

Juliana and Denise looked like sisters. They both wore their brown hair long and straight. Juliana's had a hint of natural auburn. They were the same height, nearly six feet tall, and athletic. They looked even more alike since Juliana moved to Burbank and adjusted her wardrobe to the latest local styles.

"How are you, Jules?"

"I'm good, thanks," Juliana replied. "I drove around town trying to find more stores. I'm getting pretty good at finding my way around."

"It's about time you learned the area," Denise told her. "It's been, what, almost four months since you moved here?"

"Yeah, yeah," she replied, "I'm a slow learner." Changing the subject, she asked, "How do you like my new dress?" She spun around and modeled it for her friend.

"I like it. It makes you look skinny," Denise replied. "Don't stand so close to me, you'll make me look fat."

"No way, babe, you do not look fat."

"Hey, Aunt Julie," Brandy called from the family room, "Wha'sup?"

"Nothing. Wha'sup with you?" Juliana replied.

"Nothing," Brandy said. "I'm just hangin' out with the parents."

Brandy sat on the floor with her long black hair pulled back in a pony tail. She no longer hid behind her bangs, like she did at the base. She became confident and outgoing now that she had parents that cared about her. Of all the young clones, Brandy, who was thirteen, needed a stable home and loving parents. Denise and Donald were perfect for her. Denise, like Juliana and the other staff members at the base, got to know each of the clones and understood all that they went through. And Donald had experienced the same personal discovery and social development that Brandy did. Brandy had a loving family, and a pretty cool "Aunt."

Juliana saw Brandy playing a video game with Donald. She pointed at the TV and asked, "How're you doing?"

"I'm kickin' Don's butt in Madden NFL," Brandy replied. Donald wasn't much of a match for Brandy when they played video games. He tried to play well, and over time got better, but was still far from Brandy's level of play. She didn't mind; she liked having someone to play the games with, and to beat. "He's such a noob," she teased Donald.

"I'm not a noob!" Donald protested. "I just don't understand all the rules and the plays. And the buttons confuse me."

Brandy rolled her eyes toward Juliana, shaking her head with a grin.

"Donald, you're a noob," Juliana told him with

a wink.

"We have an hour or so before dinner," Denise called out. "Brandy, can you turn off the game please? Thank you." Turning to Juliana, she asked, "Do want to sit outside on the balcony? It's not too windy this afternoon."

"That sounds good. That'll be nice," Juliana responded. "Can I help with anything?"

"Of course, you can make the coffee," Denise replied with a big smile on her face. Making coffee was a running joke with her and Juliana after spending those many weeks with Martha at the base. Juliana was Martha's assistant barista.

The two ladies led Brandy out to the balcony. Denise carried a tray of drinks; iced tea mixed with lemonade. Donald followed up with chips and salsa. They all took seats and relaxed in the warm California sun.

"So, Juliana, how's the new office?" Donald asked. "Are you learning how to process intelligence?"

"Yeah, I'm finally getting the hang of it. And I have a good friend to help me," she replied, smiling at Denise. "How's the archive group?"

"I like it," Donald replied. "I get to see a lot of documents pass by my desk. I don't have time to read them all, but I sneak a peek where I can. I'm learning little bits here and there. I like learning all that new stuff." He smiled with pride and added, "And I'm learning to type!"

"Good for you," Juliana replied. "Maybe you'll type faster than me soon. Of course, that won't be hard." She leaned over toward him and said, "I suck at typing."

"Oh! I forgot to tell you, Jules," Denise

excitedly jumped in, diverting the subject. "Brandy's moved into an accelerated learning program at school. We're so proud of her."

"Mom!"

"Don't you think that's something to be proud of?" Denise asked Brandy.

"Well, yeah, but you don't have to, like, go blabbing to everyone."

"Sweetie, this is Aunt Julie. It's not like she's some stranger at Albertson's."

"Yeah, well…"

"How is school going, Brandy?" Juliana asked. "Not grades, because I know you're doing really well," she said, pointing at Denise, "but, you know… do you have a lot of friends?" she asked sincerely.

"There are some nice girls at school," Brandy replied. "A couple live here near here, so we hang out."

"Any boys?" Juliana prodded with a grin.

"Eh, there are some cute ones. But mostly they're jerks or dorks."

"Let's just hope there aren't too many cute boys," Denise cautioned in an overly mother-like tone.

"Oh! You're such a pain sometimes!" Brandy shouted.

Juliana looked to Denise and said, "She's right. When did you turn into a prude?"

"I'm sorry, Brandy," Denise told her. "I just don't want you to get in any trouble. You have a lot ahead of you, your whole life. I don't want you to do things or be in situations that will hurt you or upset your future."

"I know, but jeez," Brandy said. "Lighten up."

"You do seem a bit over protective," Juliana commented to Denise. "It's not like you."

"Well... you're right. It isn't like me. I'm not my usual self." She looked at her family and best friend. "I was waiting to tell you until the time was right. I guess this is as good a time as any." She paused and smiled, "I'm pregnant."

Donald jumped out of his seat and rushed over to his wife with an ear-to-ear smile. He hugged her tightly and quietly said, "I'm so happy." After giving Denise another gentle squeeze, he pulled back to look her in the eyes. "We're having a baby! Are you excited? I knew something wasn't right these few weeks, but I didn't want to pester you. But now I know. Are you feeling okay? Brandy and I can make dinner tonight. And we'll clean up after. You should sit and rest--"

"Whoa! Hold on there, cowboy," Juliana interrupted. "She's pregnant, not dying of old age. She'll be fine for, like, six more months. Then," she grinned, "when she's bigger than a whale and can't get up from her chair, you and Brandy can do everything for her."

"Thanks. I think," Denise replied to her friend.

"My pleasure," Juliana replied with a smile.

Turning to her husband, Denise said, "And Juliana's right, dear. I'm fine. And I'm very happy."

"I'm gonna have a little brother or sister," Brandy realized.

"Sweetie, is that going be okay?" Denise asked.

"No, Mom, it's not okay. I don't approve," Brandy replied, shaking her head. "Like, duh!"

"Well, you have a say--"

"Not in whether you two have a baby!"

"I don't want that to change anything, you know... a baby brother or sister," Denise told Brandy.

Brandy shook her head, rolled her eyes, and looked to Juliana. She asked, "Does pregnancy turn a woman into a complete idiot?"

"It might. It sure sounds like it," Juliana replied, laughing with Brandy.

"Yeah, like a new baby won't change anything," Brandy said sarcastically. She looked at Denise and told her seriously, "Mom, I'm thrilled for you and Don. That's why people get married: to have a family! And yes, we're already a family. And now it'll be bigger. I'm cool with that. Really, I am. But I'm not changing diapers... ew."

"Sweetie, we love you," Denise replied. "I don't want you to think that we will love you any less with a new baby."

"I won't, Mom," Brandy reassured her. "And you, Don," she said to him, "Way to go! You're gonna be a dad!"

Chapter 6 - Just a Hunch

Dr. Jim Bailey's cell phone rang. "Ted! … Are you up front? Do I need to let you in? … I'll be right up." He hung up his cell and picked up his desk phone to call his group leaders to join him for the meeting.

Jim put on his sport coat as he walked down the hallway to the building entrance. He opened the glass doors for Ted and escorted his guest into the front conference room. Cindy Gordon, Sarah Deming and Bruno Jones followed right behind, wearing their lab coats and carrying notebooks.

Jim and his three team leaders at Manhattan Laboratory Services were the scientists that first analyzed the "goo" that appeared in September the previous year. They determined the composition of the substance and deduced its alien origin. They also discovered its unique property: cloning any mammal that made contact with it.

Ted relied on Jim and his team to come up with answers and postulate explanations for the unusual events associated with the alien substance and the eleven newly-cloned people. Ted trusted Jim, Cindy, Sarah, and Bruno. And they put their trust in Ted.

"Casual Friday is every day for you now, huh?" Sarah asked Ted. She was always quick to make a comment in any situation. And her spiked red-dyed hairstyle matched her feisty and boisterous attitude, an attitude that Ted appreciated from such a smart scientist.

"Casual?" Ted shot back with a grin. "I got dressed up for you guys." Taking a seat, he started the meeting. "Okay, I've got to go back and visit the committee soon. I need to give them an update. I have to tell them how well the clones are integrating into society. But I also want to give them a technical update. You know, maybe confuse them with data," he added with a smile. "I also have a question and maybe some new experiments for you, but more about that later," he said, brushing his comment away with his hand. "So, what's happened here in the last few months? What do you have?"

Cindy took the lead. She straightened her lab coat over her t-shirt and began debriefing Ted. "We've continued to characterize the substance. But we haven't made much progress. This stuff is so complex. It is way more advanced than what we're used to. We've identified some small protein sequences common to human proteins and some common DNA sequences, but just tiny fragments of the total. It's compatible with humans, but--"

"It ain't us," Sarah interrupted. "This goo is not human. It's alien all the way. We just can't crack its code."

"And we don't have much left. We need to save it," Bruno added.

"What do you mean?" Ted asked.

"We have a limited supply of active substance. We have a limited supply of the denatured stuff too. We just don't have much."

"Why not?" Ted inquired, with a hint of accusation.

"We didn't have a lot to start with," Bruno calmly explained. "When the pods of goo all arrived last autumn, they arrived in, like, a six to eight week period. That's it. Or at least that's how long it took to find it."

A slight grin cracked on Ted's phase and he continued, "Are you telling me, Herr Doctor Jones, that we don't have an unlimited supply from the heavens? We only have what fell to Earth in the short time last September?"

"Yes, unless you can call up the extinct aliens and have them light-speed ship some more to Earth," Bruno replied, giving Ted a smile.

Ted silently replied with a big smile of his own. He knew Bruno could take whatever crap he dished at him, but hadn't expected to receive it back. He was impressed.

"And some of the substance we do have left is not active," Jim added. "So we're even more limited."

"So we're finished characterizing the goo?" Ted asked Jim.

"No, not done," Jim said. "We just have to be smart with what we have left. We've actually started characterizing something other than the substance."

"Oh?" Ted asked.

"Sarah, do you want to explain?" Jim prompted.

"We're testing the mice, the cloned mice that transformed from the goo last year. We've been looking at the genotype and phenotype of the transformed mice--"

"The what?" Ted interrupted. "I slept in Biology class."

"Genotype, that's the genetic sequences and chromosomes of an organism, and phenotype is the observed characteristics and behavior of an animal. We looked inside the mice and out."

"And?"

"We found a lot of interesting stuff," Sarah told him. "First, as far as we can tell, from simple DNA analysis--"

"Fingerprint?" Ted confirmed.

Sarah nodded. "There is no genetic difference between cloned mice and native mice."

"Keep in mind," Jim told Ted, "we haven't completely sequenced their DNA; that would take way to long. Maybe we'll do that later."

"But what we did find," Sarah continued, "is the cloned mice have some interesting behavior traits. We found out they have an increased metabolism. Under normal conditions it's not a big difference, but they can process food more efficiently. If they get the right amount of food, they stay at about the same healthy weight as native mice. But, if we over-feed the mice, the transformed group doesn't gain weight like the others. And if we feed them cheese and nuts, the really bad stuff, they still don't gain weight. The native mice practically keel over and die with such a high fat diet." Sarah laughed at her memory of bloated, fat, lethargic mice.

"And," Cindy jumped in, "when we restrict their food, cut way back on how much we give them, the cloned mice don't lose any weight. The norml mice almost died, but the transformed mice didn't even come close."

"So why would that happen?" Ted asked the group. "Why is it an advantage? I'm assuming it's an advantage."

"It is," Jim replied. "Their metabolism helps them control weight. If they overeat, they can metabolize the excess so they don't get obese. If they are under-nourished, they conserve weight. That's basic survival."

"It's actually not just basic survival," Bruno corrected his boss, "it's *advanced* survival. It's better than what native species have. They can avoid obesity *and* survive famine."

"And the UV sensitivity we detected last autumn," Sarah continued, "is probably is a defense mechanism to keep animals out of the sun. Over many generations, the species may learn to stay out of the sun to avoid sunburn or skin cancer or death."

"So the cloned mice are better than normal native mice, huh?" Ted confirmed. The others in the room nodded in agreement. "What about our friends?"

"Um…" Jim paused to think. "They probably have similar advantages, I'd think."

"You mean you guess, correct?" Ted asked.

"Yes, I can only guess," Jim admitted.

"All of our friends are not overweight," Ted told the others. "Larry lost weight. He's skinnier than the original Larry. And Janet might have dropped a few pounds. And we know that Sue and the kids eat well, but they haven't gained weight. Coincidence?"

"It's hard to say," Jim replied. "With the shorter lifespan of mice, we can test and observe, and make conclusions quicker than with humans. I don't think we can say anything about Sue and the others."

"What about the UV sensitivity?" Ted continued.

"Do they have too much sunburn or skin cancer? What about the ladies in Arizona?" Bruno asked in reply.

"No. But they wear sunscreen all the time. I told them when we relocated them. I make sure they continue to put it on. I remind them every time I see or talk to them." Ted paused a moment then asked, "So what's the next step? If we don't have a lot of goo, we can't clone many more mice to test, can we?"

"Not many, maybe one or two more. But," Sarah said with a sly grin, "we can make children."

"You're breeding them?" Ted confirmed.

"Yep!" Cindy jumped in. "We're breeding cloned mice with native mice to see what behavior traits are passed down through generations."

"What'd you find?"

"The children take after their transformed parent," Bruno answered.

"What does that mean, exactly?" Ted asked.

"They have the same behavior traits as their transformed parent," Sarah replied.

"That's phenotype, right?" Ted confirmed.

"You got it."

"No exceptions?" Ted inquired. "Every child gets the UV sensitivity and improved metabolism?"

"No exceptions," Bruno responded.

"Is there any difference if the transformed parent is male or female?"

"Nope," Sarah replied, "gender doesn't matter, male or female, same result."

"Can we expect the same from our friends?"

Ted asked the group. "Will their children inherit the special traits from the cloned parent?"

"Probably," Jim replied. "If they procreate, their children will likely have the same phenotypes as their transformed parent, regardless of the other parent. But is that likely? And will we actually find out? I don't really know the people, but aren't they old, beyond the typical or even physiological safe age to have children?"

"Janet and Martha are too old. But Sue isn't. She's around thirty. And the kids aren't too old. They'll grow up and have kids one day. And Martha can't keep a secret; she's told all the others that Pasty has a boyfriend. Who knows? And Donald is young *and* married. I wouldn't be surprised if he and Denise have a baby soon... just a hunch. So, we'll see. We may have a few little clone babies crawling around here soon."

Ted stood up and leaned his hands on the table. "Now, I have a little something to tell you. It might be related, or at least worth investigating."

"What is it?" Sarah asked.

"I stopped in Enterprise yesterday. I talked with David Hudson. He's the one watching over Sue and four of the children. He told me that Sue and the cloned kids discovered something new." To build the suspense, Ted waited for the others to reply.

"What?" Sarah finally snapped.

"The clones can read and write their own language."

"Really," Jim said frankly. "I should be surprised. But," he paused, "why am I not?"

"I wasn't very surprised about the new language either," Ted told him. "But it is a little unnerving. It's another message, I bet."

"A message, like the one Sue received when she left the base? You mean the message about the extinct alien species, right?" Jim confirmed.

"Exactly," Ted said. "But now what I want to know is what was common between last year when they got the other message and a few days ago when they realized they could write a new language?" The others shook their heads. "I'll tell you what I think: proximity."

"Huh?" Sarah asked, puzzled.

"The proximity of the clones to each other," Ted explained. "When the clones are together they get a message. Sue is with four clone kids. The five of them were together when they got the new message."

"So when they get together, they're like an antenna for messages?" Jim asked.

"I don't know. They might be, or might not. That's why I called. I want you to use your cloned mice, and maybe even the offspring, to do some experiments. See what you can find out. See what happens. Do they get messages? How do they react when put together? How many mice are required? What can the mice tell us that our friends might do, or be capable of doing in the future?"

"This is… um… rather unusual," Jim replied. "It's kind of a new thing for us."

"Do your best. You guys always do."

"Okay. We'll try to come up with studies to get some answers, if there are any."

Moving the discussion on, Ted asked, "So, when will you move on to grandchildren?"

"What?" Cindy responded.

"The third generation of mice," Ted answered. "The grandchildren of the cloned mice," he clarified.

"Oh! We've already started," Sarah replied. "We stared breeding a couple weeks ago. Come back in a month or so and we can see how the grandchildren behave."

"Okay. It's a deal," Ted told them all. "I'll be back."

Chapter 7 - Ignorant Fool

"Good afternoon, Ted," the Chairman cordially greeted his guest.

"Good afternoon, gentlemen," Ted replied. He sat in his chair and squirmed a bit to get comfortable. He felt restrained having to face the committee. He never liked talking about "them aliens" with these men. The suit he was wearing didn't help either.

The committee was chaired by General Gilmore, and included Messrs. Mason and Wright. These senior government officials and politicians were assigned by DHS to oversee Ted's actions and decisions. They ordered the containment of the clones the previous year when the new people were discovered across the country. The committee members didn't trust the clones or the alien substance, and continually feared an attack on the citizens of the U.S. They reviewed the DNA fingerprint results that Ted gave them, proving the residents at the base were identical to the people, the human beings, from whom they were cloned, but no one on the committee trusted the data.

It was this same committee that Ted disobeyed by releasing and relocating the clones a few short months previously. At the time, the committee members wanted to have Ted fired so he could never work in government again, but they knew Ted was the only person the "aliens" would trust. They needed Ted to continually monitor the situation and report back.

"Thanks for coming in today," Chairman Gilman continued. "What can you tell us about the relocated ali… er… citizens?"

"The relocated citizens have settled in well," Ted informed them. "We've had no instances of unusual events or inappropriate interactions with other people in their communities. Quite the opposite, actually, they are model citizens contributing to their communities. Suzanne and Martha have each become successful in their food service jobs. They are well-liked by customers and are receiving promotions. Janet and Larry have settled into their new jobs quite nicely. Larry has learned to drive a car and just received his driver's license. Donald has his new archivist position in the L.A. regional office. And Patsy is quite successful in her college preparation studying. She has been so successful, that she will likely start college in the fall."

"And the children?" Mr. Mason asked.

"Straight A grades for all of them. They work very hard at school. The four in Kansas all play together and have made several friends in the neighborhood and at school. Brandy, the adopted daughter of Denise, one of our employees in California, has adjusted very well in junior high school."

"What about the interactions with the married couple?" Mr. Mason continued. He looked at the papers in front of him. "They're Donald and Denise, correct?"

"Yes, Donald and Denise. What about them?" Ted countered.

"Any issues there?"

"Yes. It seems that Donald snores at night and sometimes drinks orange juice right from the carton. Denise is devastated," Ted responded with a grin. After seeing the blank stares on the committee members' faces--they obviously had no sense of humor, he back-tracked. "Sorry, sir, I was trying to make a joke. No, there are no issues with the marriage."

The chairman brought the focus back on the agenda. "What's the latest update on activities at the laboratory?"

"The lab has attempted to further characterize the substance that arrived here on Earth. They have not made much progress due to the complexity of the material. It is much more complicated than anything known here on Earth. Also, characterization is limited due to the finite amount of material."

"Please clarify," Mr. Wright requested.

"The lab does not have an unlimited supply. They only have the amount of substance that arrived here on Earth in that six to eight week period around September last year. Some of it was degraded and is useless for further study. The rest is stable and can be researched, but we can't just order up more. So the lab has to be careful with the number of tests they conduct."

"So what can they do?" the Chairman asked.

"Breeding."

"Excuse me?"

"Breeding mice. They are looking at the traits

of the cloned mice relative to native mice. And they're studying the children of the cloned mice."

"What have they found?" Mr. Mason asked.

"The transformed mice have a few traits that are different from native mice. The cloned mice have a heightened sensitivity to UV radiation. This might be a mechanism to force protection against exposure to the sun. And they have a more optimized metabolism. They don't gain weight when overeating and don't lose weight when food is withheld. They can balance their weight."

"What does this mean for the ali… citizens?" Mr. Wright asked Ted.

"I'm not sure if I can answer that," Ted honestly responded. "I guess it means that they will have to stay protected from the sun. And we can monitor their weight. We'll see if they gain weight. Maybe if they're carrying a few extra pounds they may even lose weight. We think that one person, Larry, has already lost weight."

"What about the children?" Mr. Wright continued.

"The same, I guess. Protect them from the sun and see if they gain weight. But I don't see Sue letting *that* happen."

"Not the people," Mr. Wright corrected, "the mice."

"Oh. The mice offspring retain the traits of the cloned parents in all cases, no exceptions. The cloned parent's genes must be the dominant genes."

"So what does that mean?" the Chairman asked.

"It means that the children inherit the behavior traits from the transformed parent."

"Correct me if I'm wrong, Ted," Mr. Mason

arrogantly asked, "but if the children of the aliens... er... clones inherit the new traits and not the native traits, isn't that changing how evolution here on Earth will progress?"

"Possibly, but only in a micro sense, I'd imagine," Ted answered. "Future generations of the clones may be affected, but that won't affect the overall population, since there are only eleven original clones. Or at least it won't affect the larger population for hundreds or thousands of generations. Humans probably won't be around by the time any traits from this substance and the transformed people evolve to take hold on this planet."

"So the traits are an anomaly," General Gilmore confidently concluded. "Isolated and contained. This won't become a problem, since we all know that evolution is just a theory at best."

Ted shot an expression of shock at the chairman's last comment. He whispered a response, "You ignorant fool."

"That's all the time we have, Ted. Sorry to cut your time short," the Chairman pompously called out. "Please make sure you keep us updated. Can you come back in a couple months? Sound good?"

"I look forward to it," Ted responded. He picked up his briefcase and pretended to organize his papers. Quietly he added, "Not."

Chapter 8 - We Like You

Juliana sat on the couch in Denise and Donald's condo and typed an email message:

Hello all!

I hope all of you enjoyed spring break! Things are good here in Burbank. I've settled in and only pester Denise, Donald and Brandy three or four times a week. :)

I was thinking that it's been a long time since we saw each other. We left the base in November, 7 months ago! So I asked Ted if he would pay for all of us to get together. He said he would as long as we keep costs down. So here's what I'm thinking: since there are more people in Kansas compared to the other places, and Kansas is in between us all, I suggest we meet in Kansas. It's warmer than Wisconsin, cheaper than California, and has more space than Martha and Patsy's place in Arizona. Sue, I hope that you and David will agree to host us all. Between your two houses, I hope you have enough room. What do you all think about that proposal? We could try for a few weeks from now on Memorial Day weekend, or we can do it later in June when the kids are out of school. Let me know what you prefer. I'll make travel arrangements when I hear from everyone.

Write back! I hope to see you all soon! Take care!

-Juliana

"There. That should do it," Juliana said aloud. "I wonder when the others will reply. Do you think everyone will want to meet?" she asked Brandy.

"Probably not."

"Brandy!"

"Duh! Um, hello, Aunt Julie! Of course everyone will want to meet. Jeez! You can be such a loser sometimes. I bet everyone will reply by the end of the day."

"You're right, you're right," Juliana agreed.

"I'm always right," Brandy boldly responded.

"Hah!" Juliana laughed. On the way to the balcony, she walked past Brandy and said with a smile, "Always right. Yeah, sure." When she opened the screen door, Juliana greeted her friend, "Denise, if you get any bigger you won't fit on this balcony."

Donald laughed at the comment but was quickly silenced by a slap to the knee and an evil scowl from his wife.

"I'll have you know that I am not that big," Denise argued. "I'm only at fifteen weeks. I have twenty five to go."

"I can't wait until September to see how big

you'll be then," Juliana responded.

"Some day, when you have a child, Jules, you'll appreciate how special it is to be pregnant."

"Yeah, yeah," Juliana replied, "scooch a bit, hun, I can't get through."

Again, Donald laughed. But this time, he was not silenced by Denise. To Juliana, he said, "I keep telling her how good she looks."

"Oh shut up, Donald!" Denise snapped.

"No really! I think you look great. You have the healthy glow of a pregnant woman, and your larger breasts are nice too. And don't worry; the balcony will be plenty big." He smiled at Denise until he got hit again.

"Are you a little sensitive today?" Juliana asked her friend.

"Hormones are a bitch."

Brandy approached the balcony carrying her cell phone. To her mother's relief, she didn't join the others in making pregnant-woman comments. "I'm done with homework, Mom. If Katelyn is free, can I go over to her place?"

"Yes, you can go."

"Thanks Mom," she replied while texting her friend.

"I sent the email to everyone," Juliana told Denise and Donald. "I hope they're all excited about meeting. I hope Sue doesn't mind us meeting at her house."

"Everyone will be so happy to meet. And you know that Sue will love to have us there," Donald reassured her. "If you tried to suggest someplace else, she'd probably never talk to you again," he added.

"Donald's right," Denise agreed. "Sue will love

it. And everyone will be thrilled. They'll probably reply today."

"That's what I said!" Brandy called from inside the condo. "I'm leaving, Mom. See ya! Later Don! Hasta mañana, Julie!"

Juliana said goodbye to Brandy, then turned to Denise and asked, "Why does she assume she'll see me tomorrow?"

"Because you're always here," Denise answered. Seeing the partly-offended look on her friend's face, she added, "It's okay, Jules. We like you."

Chapter 9 - A Good Idea

David walked around the house carrying pool supplies. He put them on the shelf in the garage just in time to get out of Sue's way as she skidded to a stop on her bike. "Whoa! Where's the fire, lady? What's your hurry?"

"I've gotta check email to see if all the plans are set. If everyone is coming here in two weeks, we have to be ready. We've got a lot of things to do."

"But you can slow down a little bit, right?" David asked.

"Yeah, I guess so."

"Go get changed," he told her, putting his hands on her arms to calm her. "Get your computer. Come out back and sit on the patio and relax. I'll fix you an Arnold Palmer."

"That sounds nice," Sue responded. "Thank you, David." They started walking around the house together. "Hey, is the pool ready?" she asked.

"Not yet. It has to be conditioned. The chemicals have to dissolve and mix. But it should be ready on Wednesday. I can add the acid to adjust the pH tomorrow. We'll let that sit for a day, and then we're ready to swim."

"I can't wait! I'm so excited!" She leaned over and kissed David on his cheek with a smile.

David paused, awkwardly eyeing Sue. "Uh... did you just kiss me?"

"Yes, I did. I'm really happy."

"Thank you," David responded. He cracked a genuine smile as he looked in Sue's eyes. "Go get changed and come back to the patio. Don't forget your laptop."

Responding to each of his instructions, she said, "I will, okay, and I won't." She glanced at David with a grin as she started walking to her house.

Passing through the playground, *a.k.a.* the backyard, she stopped to talk to all of the kids. It took ten minutes just to reach the house. She was out of the house in five minutes after changing clothes, her laptop and sunscreen in hand, but it took another ten to navigate back through the yard while hearing more about the kids' day. Finally she sat down at the patio table. She sprayed the sunscreen on her arms and face, turned on her laptop and sipped her iced tea and lemonade.

David came out of the house with snacks and drinks for the kids and put them on the kid's table. He sat down to relax.

Sue scanned her email messages and gave David the status report. "Okay here's a message from Patsy. She sent it late last night. And one that Juliana sent this morning. Do you want me to read these to you?"

"Go for it."

"Hello everyone," Sue began reading Patsy's

message out loud. "Martha and I are excited about meeting you all in a couple weeks. It's actually less than that now. It's getting hot here in Arizona, so it will be good to go some place cooler for a few days. I want to let you all know that I'll be traveling with a friend of mine, Richard. He and I have been study partners for a while. We met in January. Despite what Martha may have said, we're just friends.

"Just friends, huh? Sure you are, Patsy," Sue commented. "I think I believe Martha," she told David, "they're girlfriend and boyfriend."

Sue continued reading, "Richard is looking forward to meeting all of you. I told him how busy it will be with all of us, but he didn't mind. I think he'll blend in. Our flight lands early in Kansas City. I think we're the first to arrive. We can't wait to see all of you. We're so excited. We'll be counting the days. See you soon. Love, Patsy."

"Who's picking people up in Kansas City?" David asked.

"I think Juliana has cars rented. Maybe it's in her email. Here, let me read it to you."

Sue clicked her mouse to open Juliana's email message and began reading aloud, "Hi all. Okay, plans are set for the meeting in less than two weeks. We're all really excited here in California. Brandy is especially excited to see all of the kids again. And I think it will be good to actually see each other in person. I'm sure we'll all be surprised at how much we've changed.

"She has one of those winking smiley faces. Why is it a winking smiley face?" she asked David. "I wonder what she meant. Anyway, I agree with her. It will be good to actually see each other."

She continued reading, "Here are the details.

Martha, Patsy and Richard fly from Phoenix and arrive in Kansas City on Friday at eleven o'clock. Janet, Larry and Mary fly from Milwaukee to Kansas City and arrive at eleven thirty. I have rented a van for Mary or Larry to drive all six to Enterprise. Then D and D and P and I arrive in Kansas City from Burbank. We'll be there around one o'clock. We have a car to drive to Enterprise. So we should all be there by two or three o'clock. Mary, Brandy, Patsy, Denise and I all have cell phones. I've include the numbers below in case you don't have them. And I've included David's as well. You all know his and Sue's house phone numbers. If something happens during the travel, call one of us. Okay, see you soon. Love, Juliana."

"Sounds like everything is covered," David observed. "Are we sure we have room for everyone? Let's see… nine adults, so we'll need eight bedrooms. The kids are all sleeping in tents in the yard."

"Eight bedrooms?" Sue questioned.

He started counting on his fingers as he reviewed the accommodation needs. "We'll need one room for Donald and Denise, one for Juliana, one for Martha, one for Patsy, one for Richard, one for Janet, one for Larry, and one for Mary."

"No. We have to combine or we won't have enough rooms," Sue replied. "Patsy and Richard are dating. They can have the girl's beds. That's only one room for them. Larry and Janet can have the boy's room. That's only one for those two. Mary can have my guest room. Donald and Denise can have my bedroom. Juliana can have my office; we'll get a cot or something. And Mary can have your guest room."

"Aren't you forgetting someone?" David asked.

"Who?"

"You," he replied.

"Oh, yeah. I can... um... sleep on the couch," Sue suggested. "That'll work."

"You can have my room. I'll sleep on the couch," David volunteered.

"Or..."

"What?" he asked.

Hesitantly, she offered, "We can share your room."

"Hmm..." David scratched his chin and looked up to the sky. "I don't know..."

Sue put her hands together and looked at him with raised eyebrows.

"Well, okay," he said with a smile.

"I knew that kissing you was a good idea."

Chapter 10 – Amazing

The convertible roadster pulled into the parking lot at Manhattan Laboratory Services. A man in shorts and a Hawaiian print shirt got out. He put his cell phone in his pocket, adjusted his Oakley sunglasses and walked to the building. The guest was met at the door by his friend, Jim.

"Wow, Ted. You sure are enjoying life, aren't you?"

"I'm certainly not taking it seriously, Jim."

The two men entered the conference room where the group leaders were waiting. "Ladies, Doctor Jones, how are you all?"

"Ted!" they replied in unison.

"Okay," Ted began, "what do you got for me? It's been about two months. How are the little grandchildren behaving?"

"I've got to tell you, we've learned a lot. These mice are amazing," Jim replied.

"Please, tell me."

"Okay," Sarah started, "we took the three

generations of mice; the original cloned mice, their children and their grandchildren. We set up a couple skills tests. The first was a maze to run. We put a little peanut butter on cracker bits at the end."

"And?"

"Compared to normal mice, the original cloned mice learned the maze twice as fast," Sarah told Ted. "And after they mastered it, they could run it twice as fast as native mice."

"The clones' children learned the maze and could run it about fifty percent faster that their parents," Cindy jumped in. "And the grandchildren learned it even faster."

"We decided to see what two mice would do when we put them in the maze together," Bruno added. "The native mice just scurried around and got in the way of the other. But the cloned mice--"

"It was so cool!" Sarah couldn't contain her excitement. "The cloned mice actually helped each other climb the walls so one could cut across the top of the maze to get to the food."

"Interesting," Ted responded, rubbing his chin.

"We also divided one of our Plexiglas boxes with a Plexiglas wall with hole about six inches up from the bottom," Cindy told Ted. "We put the mice on one side and crackers on the other."

"Okay, I'm with you. And the results?" Ted asked.

"When we put mice in the box by themselves, they couldn't climb up through the hole to get to the food," Bruno continued. "It didn't matter how many native mice we put in the box. Not one could get through the hole. But the cloned mice did it in like a minute with just two of them. One helped the other through the hole. They did it even faster when they learned the trick. And the children and grandchildren were faster still."

"And when we put three together on one side, we saw the freakiest thing!" Cindy exclaimed. "Two mice worked to get one through the hole to get the food. Then the remaining two mice worked together to get a second mouse through the hole. Then the two on the side with the food worked together to get a mouse back through the hole to the other side to deliver food to the third mouse. They all helped each other so all three got food."

The three team leaders paused to let Ted digest all the findings they just tossed at him. Ted sat and made mental notes and then looked to Jim for a summary.

"These cloned mice and their offspring can do incredible things when they're together," Jim said.

"So the cloned mice learn really fast, and they help each other when two or three of them are together," Ted said. "And the children of the clones and the grandchildren can do things even faster. And all of them are more efficient than native mice. Correct?"

"Yes, but it's not just more efficient," Jim told him. "It's like there's something there... something that makes them very different."

"When we last talked about Sue's ability to write and read a new language, Jim, you said something about an antenna for messages when several of the clones get together," Ted recalled. "Is the behavior of the mice the same thing? When two or three, or maybe even more get together they become an antenna for special behavior or receipt of message signals?"

"I don't know, Ted. It kind of seems that way," Jim replied. "I can't really explain it. But there's an extra something when the clones get together."

"Like you said, they're amazing."

Chapter 11 - The Big Day

Sue didn't sleep longer than an hour at a time. She kept waking up to review in her head arrival times, sleeping arrangements, sheets and towels, activities, beverages, and meals.

Even as she lay awake when the sun rose, she continued reviewing. *Do I have enough food? Yes, I think so. We may need more soda. We have enough beds. I get to stay with David.* A tingle ran through her body. It was the same tingle she got when she was close to him. She liked that tingle.

Hearing the girls in their bedroom--they were also too excited to sleep--she snapped out of her thoughts of David and returned to obsessing about the details. *The tent is ready. I've invited Susan and Petunia. Karen will be here for sure. I've got today and Monday off. The pool is ready.*

Finally realizing she couldn't review the details any more, she decided to get up. She put on a pair of cotton shorts, tied her hair up in a pony tail and walked down the hall to the girls' room. "Young ladies... will you please explain to me what is going on?" She walked into the room with a scowl on her face, but it quickly melted to a smile when she saw the surprised look on the girls' faces. "I'm just kidding. I'm not mad. I couldn't sleep either."

Kati and Violet jumped out of their beds to hug her. "Hi Mommy!"

"Good morning girls." Sue sat on one of the beds and the girls joined her. "Today is the big day. Are you excited about seeing Brandy?" she asked.

"Yeah! It'll be fun to have us all here together," Kati replied.

"I'm looking forward to talking with Brandy," Violet added.

"It'll be good for you to have time to talk with her," Sue agreed. "She's growing up fast and she's very smart. I think she'll like to have you talk with her." She hugged Violet, knowing how important it was for her to spend time with the older Brandy.

"So… who wants to go wake up the boys?" Sue asked excitedly.

In unison, the girls replied, "Me!"

"Get dressed. We'll go over. But we have to be quiet," she warned. "The neighbors will complain if we wake them up."

Five minutes later the three ladies met in the kitchen to go wake up the guys. Knowing it was a special day, the girls dressed in more dressy shorts and tops, instead of football clothes. Sue chose a print top to wear with her shorts, instead of a t-shirt. They each put on sunscreen and drank a glass of orange juice.

"Ready?" Sue asked the girls.

"Yeah," they replied, "let's go!"

They opened the front door and stepped out

into the bright morning sunlight. Sue closed the door behind her and started walking to David's house, but then stopped. She was surprised to see David and the boys walking toward her.

"Hi!" Kati shouted, as she ran to the boys.

"Shhh!" Sue scolded as she chased Kati and Violet, trying to keep up. When they all met in the middle of the yard, she dropped her voice to a whisper and asked Kati, "Do you want to wake up everyone in the neighborhood?"

"Sorry Mommy," Kati whispered. "I forgot."

"It's okay, Sue," David told her. He laughed and added, "Hell, the whole town knows we have guests coming today. You told every customer at the café. And everyone on the block has either donated tables or chairs, or at least been warned."

"You're right," Sue admitted. "But please don't shout," she told the kids.

"Where do you want to have breakfast?" David asked Sue.

"We can use my kitchen."

"Why do I even ask?" David smiled.

They all walked back to Sue's house to have breakfast. The kids ran off to play upstairs as David assisted Sue.

"I'm so glad Ted built this house with lots of space in it. When we get together, it gets full fast," David noted. "At least the kids still all play together. But soon Zach and Violet will want their own space."

"Zachary sooner that Violet, I imagine, but not by that much," Sue told him. "Violet mentioned to me that she wanted time to talk with Brandy. I think she wants a more mature person to talk to."

"I guess that's understandable," David replied.

When breakfast was ready, the kids were called to eat. "And I'm glad Ted built this house so sturdy," David commented, hearing the thundering herd stampede downstairs.

"Can we go swimming?" Kati asked before even sitting down.

"No, you can't. We have too many things to do before our guests arrive," Sue told her. "This afternoon you all can go swimming." She gave each of the children a plate of scrambled eggs and toast.

When Sue handed David his plate and set her plate down to eat, she asked him, "Did you turn on the pool heater?"

"Not yet. I'm letting the sun warm the water a bit before I turn on the heater."

"It'll be warm on time, right?" Sue asked nervously.

"Yes, it will," David calmly reassured her. "Everything will be ready."

"We have to set up the tables and chairs, and get ice for the coolers, and get the soda ready and--"

"Sue, please relax. We have tons of time. And we've got everything we need," he told her. He took her hands in his and looked in her eyes. "Enjoy the moment."

"You're right," Sue admitted. "But I want everything to be perfect."

"It will be, Sue. It will be." David guided Sue to sit down and eat her breakfast. He sat next to her. As they ate, he asked, "Did anyone notify Ted? Does he know that you all are meeting?"

"I don't know," Sue replied with a worried expression. "I didn't look that carefully at the emails. I think Juliana included him. Maybe Mary told him. I should ask. Do you think I should call and ask? Have their planes taken off? I can probably call Denise in California."

"Sue," David said, placing his hand on hers to get her to calm down, "I'm sorry I asked. I'm sure someone has notified Ted. Please eat. After breakfast we'll go outside. We can *slowly* get things done. And we can sit and *relax*."

Taking the suggestion from David, the kids finished their breakfast and ran outside to play.

"No playing football, girls!" Sue called before they reached the door.

"You too, boys!" David added.

David and Sue crossed paths several times as they moved between the table, sink and dishwasher cleaning the kitchen. They made contact often. Every time they rubbed hips or bumped elbows, Sue got that tingle again and liked it. After several rubs and bumps, she felt her face flush with warmth and couldn't take it any longer. She stopped cleaning, turned David around by his elbow and faced him. She didn't need to say anything. David knew. They held each other and kissed.

Chapter 12 - Guests

"Is everything ready? Where are they? It's one o'clock. They should be here already. I hope they're not lost."

"Sue, please come in the back and sit down. Relax. Pacing back and forth in the driveway won't make them arrive any faster." David tried guiding her to the back, but she wasn't moving. "C'mon. We have drinks and snacks ready."

"Is that a van?" Sue asked excitedly. "I think so. I think that's them! It is!"

The white van pulled into the driveway. The driver knew which driveway was David's because Sue was standing at the road waving excitedly. The van pulled to a stop at the garage. Larry and Mary got out of the front. Janet, Martha, Patsy and Richard got out of the back.

Sue immediately ran up and hugged Martha. "I'm so glad you're here! Welcome to my home!"

"We're glad to be here, Sue," Martha told her. "It's been so long since we saw each other."

"You look so good!" Sue told her. Seeing Martha's lightly tanned skin, and her jeans and Sun Devils t-shirt, Sue added, "You look so... happy and... and young! You look wonderful!"

"I feel wonderful," Martha proudly replied with a big smile.

Sue welcomed each of the other guests and hugged each of them, including Richard, whom she had just met. "I hope your plane flight was okay," she said to all. "C'mon out back. We have drinks and snacks waiting."

"Ahem," David uttered.

"Oh, you are so rude, Sue!" she scolded herself. She took David's arm and proudly announced, "Everyone, this is David. You've heard all about him from my emails. He's Zachary and Tyler's father."

"Thank you, Sue," David replied. He looked at the group of guests and said, "It's nice to finally meet all of you."

"C'mon!" Sue quickly took Martha by the arm and led her to the backyard while the other visitors stayed out front to greet David.

Patsy and Richard shook David's hand. Patsy was still as fit as when she first arrived. Studying hard for the GED didn't leave time for lying around being idle, and her preferred mode of transport around campus was her bicycle. She kept her sandy blonde hair cut short like Dana, her "other person" from whom she was cloned. Shorts and a t-shirt was her preferred attire, the same for most ASU students.

"We've heard so much about you from Sue," Patsy told David. "And it's all good."

"And Sue has told me all about you," David replied to Patsy. "You, on the other hand," he said, turning to Richard, "we don't know a lot about you. I hope you're ready for a lot of questions, especially from Sue."

Richard, like his study partner, was tall, thin and fit. When he wasn't in classes, he was either studying or riding his bicycle to Cupz to visit a particular barista when she was working. His blonde hair was short and somewhat messy. He wore sandals with cargo shorts and a faded t-shirt. He looked like he belonged with Patsy. "I'm ready," Richard confidently replied to David's warning. "Patsy told me I should expect a lot of interrogation. She also told me that everyone would just be curious. It's not like I'm meeting her parents."

Patsy put her hands on Richard's shoulder and told him, "I don't know, Sue and the others may make you feel like you're in a parental inquisition."

"Good luck," David told Patsy and Richard with a smile. "And welcome to our home."

"Thanks," they replied together. They smiled at each other as they walked, arm in arm, around the garage to the backyard.

Janet and Larry greeted David next. Janet wore a colorful print shirt and matching pants. She was about as old as Martha, but nowhere near as tanned. Larry wore jeans, a white t-shirt and his prized Pioneer Hi-Bred Seed hat. The two clones had relocated to Wisconsin together, where Ted found Janet a job working in a cheese shop and Larry a farmhand job on a small family farm. Although they weren't married, they behaved like a couple. They had shared the same experiences in their short lives so far and enjoyed each other's company.

"Thanks for agreeing to all this here chaos," Larry told David as he shook his hand. "I haven't been with this many people together in one place since we left that base there last November."

"And there are more people on the way," David told him.

"I can't believe we're all going to be back together," Janet added. "This will be a real treat. Thank you for offering your house."

"It's my pleasure," David replied. "This will be one memorable weekend."

Finally, Mary greeted David. She was the eldest in the group, but she, too, had a certain level of energy. After the clones were released, Mary retired. But even though she was retired, Ted asked Mary to continue to keep an eye on Janet and Larry. Her first task, once she relocated to Spring Green, was to teach Larry how to drive a car. Beyond that, she helped get them settled into their jobs and society. In the past few weeks, she hadn't needed to do much at all for her friends, and that suited her just fine.

"This all must be a little intimidating, yeah?" Mary asked David.

"So far this weekend isn't intimidating at all," he replied. "After living for seven months with Sue and the kids, not much remains intimidating. I've been conditioned."

"You're a good man," Mary said.

"And you're a good friend to all these people," he replied with a smile. "Shall we go out back and relax?"

"I think we should." She and David turned and walked to the backyard.

Mary was impressed with the number of tables and chairs set up around David's patio. Each table had a tablecloth on it, as well as glasses for drinks and bowls of snacks. There were two large stainless steel tubs filled with ice and soda. And, of course, the kids were playing football in the yard.

Sue called out, "Kati! Violet! What did I tell you about playing football in those clothes? Now, please come here and meet our guests. You too, boys."

During the arrival of the first group of guests, Sue had missed the appearance of Karen from across the street. Sue smiled and included Karen in her instructions, "And yes, you too, little sister. Please come here and meet our guests."

The kids stopped playing and walked over to the adults sitting at the tables.

"Kati, Violet, look at how big you are!" Pasty greeted the girls. "And Tyler, you've grown 6 inches at least," she added. "And who is this? David, do you have a brother? This young man is too old to be Zachary."

"No, that's Zachary," David responded with a smile of pride.

Patsy gently pulled Richard over and introduced him to each of the kids.

The children each said "Hello" to Richard and then greeted the other clones and Mary.

"Sue, did you gain an extra daughter?" Janet asked with a smile.

"Daughter? No," she replied, bending down to hug Karen. "This is my little sister, Karen. She taught me everything I knew when I first arrived. I know I told you all about her before."

"Only about a thousand times… every day," Larry said with a smile.

Everyone laughed along with Larry, remembering how much Sue talked about "her family" back in Kansas when she was first brought to the base with the others.

The kids returned to the yard to play. The adults got something to drink and then sat around the largest table to talk.

"David, I cannot believe what a wonderful yard and house you have here," Mary said. "And Sue, I assume you are to thank for all of the food and refreshments?"

"And David, of course," she smiled.

"And you have a pool? Huh… Was that here before?" Patsy asked, feigning innocence. She had a sly grin on her face, already knowing the answer.

"I think we know where that came from," Mary interjected, also with a grin. "Ted paid for it."

"I know, but I wanted to make fun of Sue," Patsy replied. Sue can get anything from Ted," she commented with a hint of envy. "What do you think, Martha… should we ask Ted for a car? Or maybe, matching motorcycles! What do you think?"

"Good idea!" Martha agreed. "Let's ask!"

"I think we need a vacation home in Florida," Janet suggested, joining in to tease Sue. "Do you agree Larry? Let's ask Ted."

"Okay, okay," Sue said. "You all know it's for the children. We have four kids, five if you count Karen. The pool is necessary."

"We're just kidding, Sue," Patsy told her. "Actually, we're all kind of jealous. You have the amazing ability to get things from Ted so easily."

"Speakin' of new things, can we see the new house, Sue?" Larry asked.

"Sure! Let's go," Sue excitedly replied.

They walked through the football field and

around the pool to Sue's house. Sue called "time out" to avoid any of the guests being injured by the game. She opened her front door and let the others inside. They walked through the hall and admired the kitchen first. The guests were quite impressed with the stainless-steel appliances and granite counter tops. Janet and Denise commented on how big the kitchen was and how much room she had. They explored the rest of the house, upstairs and downstairs, and during the tour, Sue pointed out where people would sleep.

As they exited the house, Sue halted the game again to allow the guests to pass across the football field. They all took their seats back at the tables on David's patio.

A few minutes later Susan and Petunia walked around the house. Sue jumped up and greeted her neighbors. She introduced them to her out-of-town guests and they all sat down to finish their refreshments.

The next half hour passed with everyone getting caught up with the happenings in Kansas, Wisconsin, and Arizona.

Richard had been sitting quietly, listening to the others. Sue wanted to bring him into the conversation. She said, "So, tell me about you, Richard,"

"I'm a sophomore at A-Z State, obviously. What other college is there in Tempe? I'm studying chemistry. I met Patsy in the library. Well, actually, I met her at Cupz, but she didn't really meet me. She just made my coffee. She was so busy I don't think she noticed me, he told the group, "but I couldn't take my eyes off her."

"Oh, I noticed him," Patsy added with a twinkle in her eye. "Yeah, I definitely noticed him," she repeated. "But he's right, I was too busy to talk. I never got his name, so I was really glad he helped me in the library, so I could meet him."

"So we started studying together," Richard continued. "She's really smart, even though she's not yet in college."

Patsy immediately interjected, "I will be in the fall semester."

"Did you pass the GED test?" Sue asked excitedly.

"Yep! I did!" Patsy proudly replied.

The whole group happily congratulated Patsy.

"She studied so hard," Martha told Sue and the others. "She learned all that stuff so fast. I was so impressed. I still am. She's very smart."

"So what are you going to do now that it's summer? You aren't still in school, are you?" Sue asked.

"No. But I'm still working," Patsy said. "I'll never leave my job. I love working with Martha. And Richard and I hang out at Cupz to read and stuff, even when I'm not working."

"Good luck to you in the fall," David wished Patsy. The others also passed along their good wishes.

A car pulled into the driveway, but no one out back of the house noticed right away. Only when the riders got out and closed the car doors did David and Sue notice. They jumped up to meet the newly-arrived guests. Sue ran around the corner of the house and met the California travelers on the side of the garage. Those still in back heard the squeals of delight from the side of the house. They also heard Sue shout, "Wow! Congratulations!"

As everyone in the backyard saw Denise walk

around the corner, they gasped and cheered. They offered her and Donald their congratulations.

"Okay, okay," Denise said to all, "as you can see, I am pregnant. It's been a little over twenty weeks. I'm half way there. I have about eighteen weeks to go."

"And she's only half as big as a house," Juliana added.

"I hope you have extra wide chairs, Sue," Donald chimed in.

Juliana and Donald laughed among themselves. They still enjoyed making comments at Denise's expense. Denise had even begun to laugh at her best friend and husband. She knew their comments were made in good fun.

"We don't know if it's a boy or girl and we don't want to know," Denise continued. "Baby and Mom are healthy. Okay, that's done. Now we can talk about something else."

David suggested they all take seats and have refreshments. The adults returned to the tables while Brandy joined the other children in the yard. Donald, Denise, and Juliana met Richard, Susan, and Petunia, and then all of the friends caught up with each other's happenings.

After thirty minutes of playing, the kids finally couldn't take it any longer. They begged Sue to let them go swimming. She relented and the kids scattered to their houses to get their swimming suits. Violet led Brandy to the house so she could change into her suit. In less than five minutes, the kids were standing at the edge of the pool, ready to jump in.

"Sunscreen!" David called out.

"It's in the bucket in the storage bin. Put it on please," Sue instructed.

The kids were trained well. They sprayed on the water-proof lotion and made sure it was dry before they jumped in the pool.

"They're all really well-behaved," Donald noted. "How'd you do it?" he asked.

"Ted told us we all had to wear sunscreen. There isn't any choice. So they wear sunscreen," Sue replied.

"What about Zachary?" Denise asked. "He's twelve, almost thirteen. He's getting to be a teenager. How does he have such good behavior?"

"One word: David," Sue replied. "Would you disagree with him if you were twelve?"

Looking at David's height, physique, and gruff appearance, the others understood how imposing he could be.

"It's true, I can be intimidating," David said. "But I don't have to be. Not with these kids. They're all well-behaved."

"David's actually a big puppy dog," Sue whispered to the others. "He hardly ever raises his voice."

"Since these kids have only been around for nine months," David continued, "I don't think they really know how to behave badly. Maybe I'm naïve. Maybe they'll change as they meet other kids and get older."

"What about Brandy?" Sue asked Denise.

"She has her moments, but nowhere near as bad as other kids her age. She's very well-behaved too. Donald and I are lucky. I hear what other parents say about their own children and what Brandy says about other girls. I can't believe what some kids get away with. Thank goodness Brandy isn't anything like that."

"She's a good student too, isn't she?" Patsy confirmed.

"She was in accelerated classes in second semester. She got straight A's," Denise proudly replied. Everyone agreed it was special for Brandy to be such a good student. "But don't make a big deal out of it, okay?" Denise told the others. "She's a little too modest. She shouldn't be. But she gets sensitive when I praise her. I don't mean to embarrass her, but I guess I do."

"How did the boys and girls do this year in school?" Juliana asked Sue.

"Straight A's too," Sue boasted.

"I bet you are both really proud," Martha said.

"We are," Sue and David replied.

No one noticed the convertible sports car pull into the driveway or heard the driver's door close. No one saw the man in the khaki shorts and Hawaiian shirt walk from the driveway around the garage. The assembled guests and hosts finally saw him when he came around the corner into the backyard. In unison, everyone shouted, "Ted!"

Chapter 13 – Oh

After dinner, the kids went back to the pool to swim while the adults sat on the patio and talked. As expected, Martha suggested coffee for all.

"Coffee?" David asked, surprised at the suggestion. "Isn't it a little hot yet for coffee? And it's only six-thirty. It's still sunny and eighty degrees outside."

Juliana reminded David that Martha really likes coffee. Sue reminded David that she had previously reminded him that Martha *really* likes coffee.

"Jules…" Denise added with a wicked little smile, "Why don't you help Martha?" Under her breath she laughed and whispered, "Make fun of me being pregnant, I'll have you making coffee all weekend."

Juliana replied, "What a good idea." And she meant it. She was honored to be Martha's assistant. "But I suggest we wait 'til dusk when it gets a little cooler."

Ted jumped in the conversation and asked Donald how he liked his new job in the archive group.

"I like it a lot!" Donald replied. "They're teaching me lots of new stuff, not just my job, but also courses, like communication courses and things like that. I'm even learning to type on the computer. Not just one-finger typing, but real typing." He added, "The quick brown fox jumps over the lazy dog."

"Huh?" Janet responded. "What's that mean?"

"It's a sentence that has every letter in it," Donald replied. "So you practice with it to learn where all of the keys are on the keyboard. Here let me show you. Anybody have a pen?"

Ted gave Donald a pen and Donald picked up a napkin that was lying on the table next to him. The adults all gathered around Donald to see what he was doing. He scribbled characters on the paper. The characters were a mixture of swirls and squiggles. "See? Every letter," he said, as he hand-wrote the sentence.

"Oh, I see," said Janet.

"Okay, now I get it," said Martha.

"Hold it!" David interrupted. "Those scribbles look familiar. Those are the same ones you wrote, Sue." Turning to Janet and Martha, he asked, "Can you read those?"

"Yeah," the two women replied.

Ted asked for clarification, "Those letters… that gibberish on the paper says 'The quick brown fox jumps over the lazy dog'? And you can read that?"

"Sure," Martha replied. "Can't you?"

"No, I can't," Ted answered.

David added, "None of us can."

Denise and Juliana looked at each other with confusion. Susan and Petunia weren't sure what had happened. Mary knew something wasn't right. "What are we missing?" Mary asked.

"Sue and the other clones know how to read and write a new language," Ted replied. "Although Donald didn't know he knew how to read and write a new language until just now."

"We found out a couple months ago," David added, "when Sue and the kids were writing a story together. Sue wrote in this same scribbled language. The kids could all read it, except for Karen."

Donald looked at Ted completely perplexed. "You mean I can read this, and so can Janet and Martha and Larry and Patsy and Sue. But you can't? It's a new language?" He paused then asked one more time, hoping for a different answer, "You really can't read that?"

"No, we can't," Denise added quietly, placing her hand on his shoulder.

"Look," Juliana said as she picked up the napkin, showing it to Donald and the others. "These are not English letters. But you can read them, right?"

"Yes," they all responded.

"Now flip the napkin over." She flipped it and held it up to the light so the letters were now backwards. "Can you read that? Can you recognize these letters now?"

Everyone was silent. They all tried to read the backward symbols. But no one could. The symbols only made sense in one direction.

"What does that mean?" Janet asked.

"It's another message," Ted answered.

"This is not good," David said.

"It is not," Ted agreed.

"Wait a minute. We don't know that this is a bad thing," Denise argued. "This is the first we've seen of this. So what if they can write a different language?

We've lived with them for nine months and this is the first we've seen any new behavior from them."

Sue and the other clones glared at Denise, offended at her comments. Patsy voiced the clones' displeasure, "Why are you talking about us as 'them'? Are we somehow now different?"

Mary understood the clones' reaction and tried to diffuse the obvious tension. "This is not an us-versus-them discussion. It's not a fight. There's not a good team and a bad team. But there is a clone team. We have to recognize that."

Everyone listened to what Mary said. She was always the voice of reason. Her comments worked to calm the situation. Mary suggested they all sit down and everybody did. "Let's think about this objectively," she instructed.

When people had relaxed, she continued, "This is the second message the clones have received. The first was Sue's message, when she left the base. That message was not bad. It was the memory of an extinct species from a planet in our galaxy, a planet that may no longer exist. But that memory was not dangerous. The clones are not dangerous. We all know that." She looked around at Sue and the others. "You are still human. And we even did DNA testing to prove it."

Everyone nodded.

"So we have a new message," Mary continued. "You clones can write and read a new language. How is that different from reading and writing Spanish or Chinese? The only difference is that no one else on Earth can write or read it as far as we know."

Everyone sat in silence and considered Mary's argument. Ted raised his eyebrows and nodded. David scratched his chin and sat back in his chair. The others similarly reacted to Mary, realizing she was correct.

Out of nowhere, Richard broke the silence and started talking. "When I was growing up, my friends and I made our own language for our secret club. It was actually kind of stupid, really," he chuckled. "We wrote words backwards... e-h-t for the, k-c-i-u-q for quick... and we wrote the 'e' backwards too."

Twelve sets of eyes fixed on Richard. They looked at him like *he* was the one speaking in tongues. They were stunned and amazed: stunned because they assumed that Richard did not know about the origin of Patsy, yet was contributing to the conversation; and amazed that he was not overwhelmed and disturbed by the discussion of clones, messages, and an extinct alien species.

Richard saw their expressions and thought they were confused about what he said. So he continued, "Here, look." He took the pen and paper and wrote:

əht kciuq nworb xof dəpmuj

"See?" he asked.

The others just sat in silence, staring at Richard.

Patsy broke the silence. To the others, she said, "I know what you're thinking. You're wondering why Richard is taking this so calmly, right?"

With mouths agape, the others slowly nodded.

"I told Richard about my past before we came here," Patsy told them. "He and I are very close. He really wanted to come on this trip with me. I thought if he really wanted to be with me... you know, like, more than just a friend, he'd eventually have to find out. So I told him. The worst that could happen was that he'd think I was completely crazy and run away as fast as he could. But then he wouldn't have been worth keeping, right?"

Seeing the other's blank expressions, Patsy said, "I'll take that as a yes." Looking at Richard, she continued, "As you can see, he took the news quite well. I'll admit he was kind of freaked out for a while. But I explained what happened at the base and the DNA testing and all that. And he knows Martha and she's normal. And I showed him our emails, so he knows you all are normal. We just had a different start to life, right?"

Seeing the others hadn't changed their expressions, Richard leaned over to Patsy and said, "This is awkward."

"Tell me about it," Patsy replied. The two broke into laughter.

That was enough to shake the others from their state of confusion. They snapped back to life and started laughing themselves. They understood what Patsy had just told them; they knew Richard was now part of their circle of friends. And he had made an interesting point when he talked about his childhood club.

"Richard's right," Juliana concluded. "This new language is nothing more than a secret club language for you all. If you're not in the club, you don't know the secret language. There's nothing wrong with that. There's no harm."

A thought popped into Denise's head. "Does this mean Brandy can read it too?" Not waiting for an answer from the others, she called out, "Brandy, can you come here for a minute?"

Brandy got out of the pool and came over to the tables, drying off with a towel. Denise showed her the symbols that Donald had written earlier. "Can you read this?"

"The quick brown fox jumps over the lazy dog. What about it?"

She noticed the adults' uneasy looks and got defensive. "What'd I do? Did I do something wrong? Is this a joke?"

"No, sweetie, you read it correctly. And it's not a joke. We all just realized that you and Donald and the other clones have your own language." Denise turned the paper over, the way Juliana did earlier.

Brandy saw the backwards symbols and, like the others, couldn't read the sentence. She quickly understood the situation and said, "Oh."

Chapter 14 – Still Watching

The sun began to set and the air started to cool.

"Martha, I think it's time for coffee," Ted called out.

"I'll help," Juliana instinctively responded. She quickly stood up.

"Wow!" Patsy observed. "That was completely Pavlovian!"

Richard barked for extra effect.

"I don't get it," Brandy said, looking confused. "What's Pavlovian?"

Denise gave her daughter a quick history lesson. "There was a famous scientist named Pavlov who trained dogs to bark or drool or something every time a bell rang. He conditioned dogs to... drool, yes, it was drool, when he gave them food and rang a bell. Later he could ring the bell only and get the dogs to drool without food. Juliana is conditioned the same way: someone suggests coffee and she jumps up to help Martha. It's funny."

"Okay. Whatever," Brandy replied, rolling her

eyes.

"*I* thought it was funny," Juliana said. "And you're right, Patsy, it is totally Pavlovian. C'mon Martha, let's go. We haven't made coffee together in a long time."

Sue and David extracted the kids from the pool. Susan gave Karen dry clothes for the evening and told her to go change with the other girls in their house. Brandy followed the girls to go change also. The boys went inside their house. David told them they could all play together at Sue's house when they were dressed.

Denise stood up to start cleaning, but Donald protested. He told her to sit and, for once, she actually did. Richard and Larry assisted Donald.

Ted took the opportunity to slip out front and make a phone call. "Jim, it's Ted. ... Yes, I know it's after hours, but it's only eight o'clock. It's better to call on Friday night than on Saturday or Sunday, right? ... Listen, I have to tell you something; the others can read and write the same language that Sue can. ... Yes, the clones. They're all here in Enterprise. We're having a reunion. So what does this mean? ... All eleven of the clones can read and write the language. It's another message. What can I expect them to do? ... Good things? Bad things?"

He paused and listened to Jim. "Okay. But can you guess? ... Right, now I remember. The cloned mice helped each other, getting food for the others. Those are good things. You think the same applies to our friends? ... Okay. Thanks Jim. ... Huh? ... Yeah, I am a little nervous," he admitted. "I don't like surprises. I especially don't like surprises that will get people in trouble. DHS is still watching. If this message leads to something bad, we'll all be in hot water. I don't want that."

He patiently listened as Jim shared his thoughts. "You're right, Jim. It's like Spanish or French; just another language. You've been a big help, Jim. Thank you. … I've got to get back to the party. We'll talk again soon. … I appreciate your help. Thanks a lot."

Ted hung up and joined the others in the back yard as the first round of coffee was served. Juliana and Martha handed out cups, and then went back inside to make another two pots, but not before Martha commented, "Sue, I thought you would have had a professional coffee and espresso maker like me."

"No, I'm sorry, Martha. I just have a regular coffee maker. But at least I brought mine over to David's house so it'll go faster."

"Thanks, that helped," Martha replied as she closed the screen door.

"David, where are the tents?" Susan asked. "Aren't the kids going to sleep in tents out here in the back? Shouldn't we set them up?"

"Sue and I set them up in the garage earlier today. We'll bring them out when the kids are ready. We have sleeping bags, too."

"Good thing it's warm outside," Petunia added.

Juliana and Martha came back outside after setting the two machines to brew more batches. They sat down with the others.

"I can't help but wonder…" Mary began, "the message… the new language… why didn't it come to you earlier?"

"I don't know," Donald replied. "Why did it come to me today, of all days?"

"And why did it come to Sue a couple months earlier?" David asked.

No one could answer either of the questions.

Richard asked the group, "When did Sue's message come to her last year? Is there a connection between the two messages?"

"We were all sitting around talking about the Earth," Mary recalled. "I think we were talking about plate tectonics, the planet core, and the atmosphere."

"You said the planet was dying," Sue reminded her. "I said it was not."

"So was it the subject of the conversation that triggered the new message?" Richard asked.

"Maybe," Mary said.

"But why would the topic of Donald learning to type or Sue playing a game with the kids trigger a new language?" Denise asked.

Again, no one had any answers, except Ted. He had been standing behind the others, so they couldn't see his confident grin. He finally spoke. "What was common to both situations?" Ted asked.

The others turned to look at him. He had a look in his eyes that showed he had an explanation. "Anyone?"

No one responded.

"All of you were together in both cases. Or at least more than four of you were together," Ted said. "You get messages when enough of you clones are together."

"Interesting… proximity is the trigger," Mary said. "Interesting."

"So are you saying that when enough of us get together, we're like a satellite dish to receive messages from outer space?" Patsy asked for clarification.

"Who knows where the message is coming from?" Ted asked rhetorically. "It may be coming from outer space, and all of you cloned from the alien goo can detect it. Or maybe the messages are internal to you, from the goo itself, and you just need enough people to bring it to the surface."

"What do you know that you're not telling us, Ted?" Mary asked.

"I asked our friends at the lab to do some experiments with the mice that were cloned in the lab from the goo. I had an idea that proximity was the trigger. They confirmed it."

"How?" Patsy asked.

"Individually, the cloned mice didn't do much different than normal mice. They did things faster, but nothing much different. But when the lab put two or three cloned mice together, they acted very differently. They did some pretty amazing things. The group of cloned mice had a different purpose than a single mouse."

"So you really think that being together triggers these messages?" Patsy confirmed.

"Yes," Ted answered. Then a sly little smile broke on his face and he added, "So... you know what that means?"

"Don't you dare keep us apart, *Mister Stevens*!" Sue shouted.

The others, shocked and amazed, stared at Sue. She had an expression so intense it would melt ice.

Ted, however, was calm and collected. "How did you know what I was going to say?"

"I know you, Ted," Sue replied. "I know you."

"You do indeed, Sue," Ted quietly agreed. "However, I was not serious. I was only going to joke about keeping you all apart. In fact, I'm very interested in learning more about this phenomenon."

"Well, maybe we'll surprise you this weekend," Sue announced, cooling down several degrees. "Maybe we'll receive a whole bunch more messages."

"Maybe you will," Ted said with a smile.

The sun finally set and it started getting seriously dark in the yard. David turned on the outdoor lights in the backyard and asked Sue if she'd help with the tents. Together they brought a tent out from the garage. Larry and Richard brought out the other. Donald, Janet and Patsy carried sleeping bags and placed them in the tents.

When they all sat back down, Martha and Juliana refilled coffee cups. Sue, having regained her composure, asked if they all wanted to know where they were sleeping tonight. They all agreed, so Sue listed the arrangements. "Patsy and Richard will sleep in the girl's room in my house. I hope you don't mind pink. Denise and Donald can have my room. I have a queen-sized bed. Martha can sleep in the guest room and Juliana can sleep in the office. Larry, you and Janet can sleep in the boy's room in David's house. We have a bed for each of you. And Mary, you can sleep in David's guest room."

"Wait," David interrupted. "What about Ted?"

"Don't worry about me. I can get a hotel or something," Ted replied.

"You will not," Susan protested. "You can sleep in my guest room. You don't mind a little walk across the street to my house, do you?"

"I don't mind at all," Ted replied. "Thank you, Susan."

"What about you, Sue?" Patsy asked. "You don't have a room."

"Me? Oh, I'll sleep on David's couch." She

fidgeted nervously and looked down at the ground.

"There's no need to be embarrassed," David told her quietly.

The others looked at the two of them in confusion.

"Oh, okay…" Sue said, blushing for the first time in her life. "David and I will share his room tonight."

The ladies gasped and squealed like teenagers at a sleep-over. The men whooped like fraternity brothers at a bachelor party. Everyone was happy for Sue, including Sue.

Chapter 15 - Meant for Us

"Honestly, Mommy, we tried to be quiet. We really did."

"Kati's right, Mom. We did our best to stay quiet as long as possible," Violet added.

"Zach and I did too, Dad," Tyler told David.

Sue and David stood in between the two tents in the backyard, their hair messed and their eyes still groggy. David had on shorts, but no shirt. Sue had on her night shirt and a pair of David's sweatpants. They each wore a scowl on their faces. "It's six-thirty," they said in unison, trying to keep their voices down.

"It's hard to sleep when the sun comes up, Sue," Karen said. She was trying to objectively defend her fellow children.

"I'm sure it is, little sister, but you can still be quiet, can't you?"

Karen quickly lost the debate. She lowered her head, as ashamed as the others.

"Stay in your tents," Sue instructed. "If you all want to sit in one tent, that's okay. It's up to you. But you *must* be quiet. We do not want to hear you again. Not for another hour. If David and I can hear you, so can everyone else. Your tents are in between the houses. Don't wake up our guests. Brandy, you're the oldest, so you're in charge."

Sue and David turned and slowly walked back to his house. "Coffee?" he asked her.

"Is it too late to go back to bed?" Sue coyly suggested.

"We won't get any more sleep," David concluded.

"I don't want to sleep," she smiled. "I just want to hold you."

But it wasn't meant to be. Donald and Denise walked out of Sue's house, followed by Juliana, several feet behind. Like David and Sue, their hair was mussed, and they had thrown on the nearest clothes they found.

Hearing her own porch door close, Sue turned to see her three friends. She and David waited for their guests to reach them in the yard. "Good morning," Sue whispered.

"Morning," Denise replied.

Donald grunted.

"Why are you up? Did the kids wake you up? I'm so sorry they were noisy," Sue apologized. "We told them they had to be quiet. But you know kids."

"No, the kids didn't wake me up. It's my bladder."

Sue looked at her confused.

"The baby… it pushes on my bladder. I have to pee a lot. I usually wake up early," Denise told her. "But it sure beats morning sickness," she added. "That was the worst."

Donald grunted again.

"Morning," Juliana mumbled as she finally reached the others.

"Your bladder isn't waking you up too, is it?" David joked with Juliana.

"Ha. Funny," Juliana sleepily replied.

"C'mon," David said to all. "We'll get some coffee brewing."

They walked to David's house and entered the kitchen through the screen door. The Californians took seats and silently waited. Sue and David made coffee as quietly as they could.

After the first slug of caffeine was infused into the guests from Burbank, they started to liven up. Juliana started in with the pregnancy comments. "So, the bladder woke you up this morning, huh? I figured you'd be, like, capsized on one side and woke up 'cause you weren't able to roll over."

"Ha ha. Funny Jules," Denise blandly replied. She wasn't as awake as her friend, but still defended her honor. "I'm not even that big yet. I can still roll over just fine as long as Donald isn't snuggled up next to me."

"Speaking of snuggling..." Juliana quickly chose her next victim. "How did you two sleep?" she asked Sue and David with a wicked smile.

"Fine," David replied, not revealing too many details.

"I had no trouble rolling over," Sue added, "even with David snuggled up next to me." She returned the smile to Juliana.

Juliana started to cackle loudly at the thought of Sue and David's new relationship, but quickly slapped her hand over her mouth. "Shoot! I hope I didn't wake the others," she whispered. "Do you have any more coffee?"

"I think you've had enough already, Miss Spastic," Denise replied.

As Juliana suspected, she heard movement and talking in the other side of the house. She heard a toilet flush. "Hey, someone else is pregnant," she laughed.

Denise slapped her on the arm.

Mary, Janet, and Larry entered the kitchen from the hallway.

"Oops," Juliana told them. "Sorry guys. I didn't mean to wake you."

Larry told her not to worry about it. Janet and Mary quietly agreed.

Martha, Patsy and Richard surprised the others by entering the kitchen from the backyard a few minutes later.

"I know I didn't wake you guys up," Juliana said, pointing at the new arrivers. "Or did I?"

"You didn't wake us," Patsy told her. She turned and looked to Sue, "But six little pixies did."

"Oh no," Sue replied. "I'm so sorry. We told them to be quiet. I'll go take care of this."

"Sue, let it go," David said. "We're all up now. Let them play."

"Yeah, Sue," Patsy added. "They're just kids. They're having fun. You can't expect six kids to be quiet for that long. And David's right, we're all up now."

"Where's the coffee?" Martha tersely asked.

"Coming right up," Sue replied.

As Sue handed out coffee to her guests, the kids came storming in the house. "When's breakfast, Mommy?" Kati asked.

"Coming right up," Sue replied. Her response was part Pavlovian and part stampede-control. "But you kids have to eat outside."

"Do you kids want some orange juice while you're waiting for breakfast?" David asked.

"Sure," Karen replied.

"Mom, Brandy told us that you… well, all of us, I guess… know a different language," Violet said. "Is it the same one we wrote that one night? She said it was another message, like the one you got last year."

"Was that the one about the extinct people from another planet?" Karen asked excitedly. "Maybe the language is an *alien* language. Cool!"

"Hold on there, little lady," David told her. "Before you get all excited, we don't know what it means." Looking to the others, he asked, "Does anyone know what it means?"

No one had an answer.

"So until we know what it does mean, Karen… and all of you kids… let's not say anything, shall we?"

"Okay," Karen replied.

"But why did we get the message now?" Brandy asked. "Why didn't we each realize it sooner?"

"We don't know for sure," Denise replied.

"Ted thinks it has to do with how close you all are," Mary added. "This is the first time so many of you clones have been together since you all were on the base."

"When Sue got the last message?" Brandy confirmed.

"Hey," Larry addressed the others, "ya s'pose the two messages are connected? Are Sue's message and the new language related? Ya think they were meant for us?"

"Do you mean that Sue should have written her message in the new language?" Janet asked for clarification.

"No, that's not it, because she didn't know the language last year," Donald replied. "And writing in the new language wouldn't have been too effective. No one could have read it."

"Maybe we should write down Sue's message about the extinct species in the new language," Martha suggested.

"What good would that do?" Brandy asked. "To, like, save it?"

"That's an option, I guess. But if no one can read it, why save it?" Patsy argued. "We'd have to translate the message. Why not just write it in English?"

"Maybe we're supposed to *do* something," Brandy offered. "Maybe we're supposed to write about the environment. Maybe we should write about our planet so that we don't end up like the other planet."

Everyone in the kitchen stood in silence, thinking about Brandy's idea. They knew, somehow, that Brandy was correct. No one could explain it, certainly not the non-cloned in the room, but yet they all knew Brandy was correct.

The pensive silence in David's kitchen was broken by Ted and Susan who had walked around the house and now stood at the back screen door. "Good morning everyone, I see you're awake bright and early this morning," Ted said.

"As are you," Denise replied.

Karen ran over to the screen to greet her mother. She opened it up and gave Susan a big hug. "Hi Mommy! We got a lot of sleep last night, I promise. We were good."

"And you just woke up, right?" Susan asked.

"Sort of," Karen tactfully replied.

"Sort of, huh?" Susan looked at Sue and asked, "Six, or six-thirty?"

"They made it to six-thirty, believe it or not," Sue replied.

"Breakfast anyone?" David asked the adults.

They all agreed, so David and Sue started moving through his kitchen preparing and serving breakfast in waves, starting with the kids.

After finishing eating, Donald and Richard volunteered to clear the table and start cleaning the dishes. The rest of the adults went outside, sat in the morning sun, and sipped coffee. Although they were served first, the children were still eating. They were busy chatting and laughing at their table. Ted asked the group what was on the agenda for the day.

"Susan has graciously offered to give us a personalized tour of her museum," Sue told everyone.

"*Her* museum?" Ted asked.

"Yes, the Dwight D. Eisenhower Presidential Library," Sue replied. "Susan works there."

"Library?" Zachary loudly complained from the kids table. "It summer vacation. I don't want to go to a library!"

"Yeah, I don't want to go. Do we *have* to?" Tyler whined.

"It's not a *library* library," Karen told the boys. "It's cool! My mom took me there once. It's full of old things about a president. There's lots of pictures and stuff, all about Ike. That's what they called the president. There are some books there too, but they're in glass boxes. You don't read them."

"I went to the Ronald Reagan Library. He was a president too," Brandy added. "We went on a field trip to Simi Valley. It was pretty cool. They have Air Force One inside."

"What's that?" Tyler asked.

"It's the President's plane, dummy," Zachary told his younger brother. "But they can't have the President's plane in the museum," he argued with Brandy.

"No, really. They have the actual plane, the *whole* plane, right there in the museum. It's not the current plane, you know, the seven-forty-seven. It's the old Air Force One, before the seven-forty-seven. President Reagan flew in it so much they let him put it in his museum," Brandy informed them. "And it's also full of stuff from, like, the olden days in the nineteen-eighties, but it's still cool."

"Is there a plane in your museum?" Tyler asked Susan.

"No, Tyler, I'm sorry to say that we don't have an airplane in our museum," Susan replied. "And yes, we have a lot of old stuff, even older than Reagan's museum. Like more than *thirty years* older," she added to see what response it would get from the boys.

The boys were polite and didn't verbally complain. But they did roll their eyes.

"It's history, boys," Susan continued. "It's the history of the United States. It may not be exciting like a video game, but it's good to see what things were like many years ago."

"It's not bad," Brandy reassured Tyler and Zachary. "You'll be okay. It's cool to see the old stuff. You'll like it."

"And you might even learn something," David

firmly suggested to his boys.

"Sounds good," Ted announced. "When are we heading out?"

"Any time," Susan replied. "We can go at any time."

"Let's take thirty minutes or so to finish cleaning and then get dressed. How's that sound?" Sue asked everyone.

Everyone agreed. They all helped clean up and then dispersed to their rooms to get dressed. Sue fussed in David's kitchen while Denise and Donald changed their clothes in her bedroom. When they were finished and returned to David's house, Sue quickly ran home, showered and got dressed.

The whole group was ready in just forty minutes, which was pretty good for nineteen people, six of whom were chatty kids with short attention spans. They climbed into the van, the Chevy, and Susan's car to haul all of them to Abilene.

Chapter 16 - She's Good

When they returned from the museum in the afternoon, the younger kids burst out of the van and ran to their rooms to put on their suits to go swimming. Brandy stayed back, joining the adults. She pulled out her cell phone to check Instagram and Twitter, and texted with her friends.

As she walked around the house with the others, Susan said "That wasn't too bad," directing her comment to Sue and David. "I thought we would have heard a lot more complaining."

"You're right," Sue agreed. "They were actually pretty well behaved. And I think they actually learned something."

"Amazing," David commented.

As they reached the tables in the back, all but David and Sue took seats. "What can we get you all? Would you like lunch or snacks?" Sue asked.

"How about just snacks now, Sue," Martha proposed. "We can have an early dinner. That's what I suggest."

The others agreed with Martha's suggestion. Donald stood up and volunteered to help get the snacks and beverages for everyone. They filled the tubs with ice and put in bottles of water and cans of soda. They brought out pitchers of lemonade and iced tea. And they brought out bowls of chips and salsa.

"Martha's going to have to teach you how to make guacamole," Patsy told Sue. "It's the best."

"It's really good," Richard added.

"Yes, she will," Sue replied. "I should introduce some authentic southwestern dishes at the café. You can give me some recipes. I'll name the dishes after you. Like, Martha's Guacamole."

"That doesn't sound too exciting," Patsy noted. "How about Guaca-martha-mole?" she suggested.

"That's a mouthful," Juliana said.

"Yeah! That's it! 'Guaca-martha-mole; it's a mouthful!' That'll be what you can say to get customers interested," Patsy suggested.

"Have you considered advertising, dear?" Mary asked Patsy. "I think you'd be really good at it."

"I know she would," Richard confirmed. "She's always coming up with new ideas and slogans and stuff. Now, some of them are pretty crazy. No offense, babe," he said to Patsy. "But then some of her ideas are really good."

"Richard!" Patsy protested, trying to be modest.

"No, really." He explained to the others, "She came up with a saying for the coffee shop, you know, Cupz, spelled with a 'z.'" He spread his arms like he was unfurling a banner and said, "'Cupz: put the zees behind you.' Get it? Zees, you know, as in sleeping. So when you drink coffee with caffeine, you don't sleep and you put the zees behind you."

"Not bad," Ted praised with a smile. "Not bad at all, Patsy."

"I really liked it," Martha said. "I told the store manager. He liked it too. We didn't make fliers or anything, but now some of the regulars say it when they walk in."

"You have a bright future in marketing," David said. Patsy blushed and thanked him.

Donald, who wasn't paying attention to the group, as he was sometimes known to do, abruptly changed the subject by announcing, "I thought it was interesting to see today how much President Eisenhower invested in military and transportation. I didn't know he was the one who built the interstate highways."

"The military-industrial complex," David added.

"Yep," Ted added. "He really built up modern industry and military after World War Two. Cars, jet planes, missiles, even rockets really took off... heh heh, excuse the pun, under Eisenhower's two terms in office."

"You mean, he's the one that started all of the pollution in the atmosphere?" Brandy asked.

Ted, David, and Mary were taken aback by the conclusion that Brandy drew. She was correct about pollution increasing, but they didn't expect her to make the connection.

"Yes, but not really," Mary replied. Seeing Brandy's confusion, she said, "Let me explain. Burning coal for electricity and power in the industrial revolution at the turn of the twentieth century started the carbon dioxide emissions. The growth after the war didn't help, but it wasn't the start. You can't blame only Eisenhower."

"But it was the U.S. who did most of the polluting, right?" Larry asked.

"Far from it," Mary continued. "England, France, Germany, Russia, India, China… any country where there's a lot of manufacturing and high population will add carbon dioxide to the atmosphere."

"So that's what you meant, Mary, when you talked last year about people destroying the atmosphere?" Janet confirmed.

"Yes," Mary answered. "But it's not intentional. People aren't trying to destroy the atmosphere, but just living and driving and having electricity for billions of people on the planet has taken its toll."

"How do we fix it?" Sue asked. "How can we repair the atmosphere?"

"It's hard to do," David chimed in. "How do you tell billions of people to stop driving and stop burning coal and oil to have electricity?"

"But *something* can be done," Donald protested.

"That's true," Mary replied. "But only a little bit can be done at a time. Like David said, you can't stop everyone on the planet from driving cars and using electricity. But, if everyone cuts back a little, and we use alternate energy like solar, nuclear, wind, and electric vehicles, and if countries pass laws to limit how much manufacturing and power companies can pollute, we, meaning everyone on the planet, should be able to clean up the atmosphere."

"Why isn't anyone doing anything about it?" Donald asked.

"Some people are trying," Mary responded. "Some people are cutting back and trying alternate energy, and some states are trying to pass laws to control carbon dioxide emissions. But until the whole country, and all countries on the planet take serious action, I don't think there will be much change in behavior."

"Nor any repair to the environment," Denise added.

"We should do something," Sue insisted.

"What do you propose?" Ted asked, interested in her ideas.

She thought for a few moments, then suggested, "We can write letters. We can warn people that Earth will become extinct if we don't clean the environment."

"I don't think you'll be very successful," Ted cautioned Sue. "There are thousands and thousands of people in the U.S. who send letters every year to whoever they can think of. Nothing happens. No one even responds. Why would your letters be different?" Ted asked.

"Well…" Sue scrunched her face, struggling to find a solution. "We could find the right person to contact. And we could write in our new language, like a code to break. That will get attention."

Ted laughed. Being in the government for nearly thirty years had made him cynical when it came to letter-writing campaigns. "I applaud your idea, but it's not going to be successful. If you send letters in a coded message to someone as high up as, say, the Secretary of the Interior, the most you'll get is the FBI investigating the code as a domestic terror threat. The letters will probably just be shredded."

"I think you're wrong, Ted," Sue told him, staring him down. "I think we can get our message to those who can help. We've done some amazing things already. Why don't you think we can do it?"

"I think you all can give it a good try, but history is not on your side."

"History is never on our side," she countered.

"True," Ted said, "but I still don't think it will work."

Sue folded her arms and pouted. She didn't like Ted telling her that they couldn't succeed. She knew that they could get the message out there. But they had to find the best way to do it.

Throughout the conversation between Sue and Ted, the others watched and listened. They could see that Sue was enthusiastic, even emphatic about the cause, and they could also see her frustration with Ted's responses.

Patsy tried to cheer her up. She lightened the mood by suggesting, "We need a slogan. Let's think about what slogan we can put in the letters."

The others quickly joined in supporting their friend. Ted quietly shook his head.

"Okay, so we need the slogan to be catchy," Patsy began. "We need to have a simple phrase that everyone can say easily and is memorable."

"Stop the pollution. It's killing the Earth," Janet proposed.

"That gets to the point, but I don't think it's catchy enough," Patsy replied. "People have to get excited about the slogan."

"What about something like 'Drive less and save electricity?' That's simple enough, ya know," Larry added.

"Or maybe 'Let's clean up the atmosphere.'" Martha offered.

"I like the idea of cleaning," Patsy said, thinking

how she could take it a step further. "What about something like 'Do your part and clean…' No, that's not it." She struggled to come up with a play on cleaning.

As the adults sat and pondered slogans, the kids whirled in from the pool, still dripping water, to get some snacks. They dug into the chips and salsa and grabbed cans of soda. Karen sat down and boldly joined the adult conversation. "So, what are you talking about?"

"Cleaning, little sister," Sue replied. "We're talking about cleaning up the environment."

Right on cue, another Pavlovian response, Katie and Violet called out in unison, "You live in this house. Clean up!" They both smiled at their mother.

Everyone looked silently at the girls, surprised by their automatic response.

After seeing the others' expressions, Violet added, "Well, that's what you tell us, Mom, when we have to clean up the house."

"That's it!" Pasty called out. "'You live on this planet! Clean up after yourself!' That's the slogan! It says that it's everyone's responsibility to clean up the planet and everyone has to do their part. It doesn't say that it's the government's problem. It says that we all have to do a little cleaning."

"That's really good, Patsy," Brandy complimented her. "I like it!"

The others all agreed. Even Ted was impressed.

Richard pointed to Patsy and called out to everyone, "See? I told you she's good!"

Chapter 17 - We Promise

The sun set after dinner and the weather was cooperating nicely. It was a clear, warm evening with just enough of a breeze to keep the bugs away. Everyone, even the children, sat in a big circle around the portable fire pit David set up. He loaded more wood on the fire and it burned brightly.

There was electricity in the air that Ted could feel. He couldn't explain it, but he sensed it was there. A force was at work that he knew was the result of having all the residents back together again. He wondered to himself just what these people could do when they put their minds together. He knew what Sue could do just by herself.

"You know," Brandy started, "there are a lot of kids at my school that would like to help with the environment, like spreading the word about cleaning up. I think a lot of kids want to do something, because, like, they gotta live for a long time. Adults may not care because they're gonna die soon. But kids care."

"I care!" Karen chimed in.

"Yeah, so do I," Zachary added.

"Maybe we should try to get the message to kids," Brandy suggested.

"That's not a bad idea," Denise replied. "We could start a campaign for schools, about how everyone should do their part."

"They did a similar thing in the eighties," Susan chimed in. "Nancy Reagan led the fight against drugs in schools. Her slogan was 'Just say no.'"

"Who was Nancy Reagan?" Martha asked.

"President Reagan's wife," Ted answered.

"Oh," Martha responded. "You mean the guy with the airplane in his library. I see. Donald Reagan's wife was Nancy."

"Ronald Reagan," Ted corrected.

"Whatever," Martha replied, holding up three fingers in a 'W', like the ASU students she served at Cupz.

"Just Say No?" Brandy asked, not recognizing the slogan.

"I've never heard of it," Patsy added.

"That's because you're too young," Susan replied. "I was barely in elementary school when it became popular."

"I remember it," David said to all. "And it worked too. It was easy to remember and got to the point. If someone offers you drugs, you just say no."

"So if someone asks what we can do for the environment, we tell them to clean up after themselves," Brandy said. "Do you think it will catch on?"

"We need some help," Sue announced. "We need Nancy Reagan."

"Uh, there's a small problem, Sue. She was very

old and she's no longer alive," Ted said. "You need to find someone else."

"So who can we find?" Brandy asked.

"Let's get the current President's wife to help," Patsy suggested.

"Hold on here folks," Ted interjected. "You can't just call up the First Lady and ask her to start a campaign for school kids to clean up the environment."

"Why not?" Karen asked.

"Yeah, why not?" Sue repeated.

Soon all the others were asking Ted the same question. Ted was barraged by the clones with appeals for an explanation.

David came to his rescue. "Look everyone. It's not as easy as you think. The President and the First Lady have their own ideas about what things they want to support. They aren't going to be influenced by a few people writing letters."

"You're probably right, David," Mary said, joining the conversation. "Cleaning the environment is not a new idea. And letters from normal citizens are not likely going to start anything. But our friends here, and no offense to anyone, are not normal," she said, looking around to the clones. "You have a message, and we all know it. Carefully planned letters suggesting a new campaign for school-age kids coming from people with the memory of an extinct species might just work."

"Mary," Ted began, "you've been retired a little too long, I'm afraid. And Janet and Larry must really be rubbing off on you after six months."

"Excuse me?" Mary shot back, offended at Ted's comment.

"If you think this has any chance of working,

you're wrong," Ted said.

"That's why it has to be carefully planned," Mary suggested. "If we just send of a couple letters to the White House, you're right; it won't work. But if we plan when and to whom we send letters--"

"We can send the letters to the President's daughters!" Brandy announced.

"See?" Mary said to Ted. "Carefully planned messages sent to the right people, maybe the President's daughters, for example, might get the message out. The First Lady will listen to her children."

"This is crazy," Ted replied to all.

"Ted," David said calmly, "maybe it's not."

"Have they already brainwashed you David?"

"Maybe Mary's right," David said. "If our friends and family were normal people, it probably wouldn't work. But they're not normal. And the government knows about them. Probably not the President, but Homeland Security does. We have an advantage. We can use it. I'm not sure exactly how, but I'm sure we can use it."

Ted sat back in his chair and all eyes were on him. He thought about Mary's and David's comments and what might be possible. He sat for several moments. His mind swirled with ideas while the little voice inside his head constantly told him it would never work. He finally spoke, "We might be able to… but that won't… and they'd… and what if…" After listening a few moments longer to the confusion in his head, he snapped out of his thoughts and said to all, "We have no idea this will even work. You'd be wasting your time and you all might get in serious trouble."

"That's true," Sue replied. "But it's our time to

waste. And if there's a chance it will work, I'm willing to try. What harm can a few letters do? Can they put us in jail for writing letters?"

"Yeah," Donald added. "They can't arrest us just for sending letters."

"I agree," Patsy said. "Let's write the letters."

The others all agreed. It was eighteen against one. And even the one wasn't sure he was against the plan.

"Ted, we promise not to do anything without checking with you. Will that be okay?" David asked.

"We promise," Sue confirmed.

"Yeah, we promise," Brandy added for effect.

Ted eyed Brandy suspiciously, eyed Sue with doubt, then looked to David for reassurance. He couldn't help thinking something would go wrong. Finally he broke. "Okay, you can write your letters."

Applause and cheering filled the night air. Everyone was enthusiastic about the plan. As a group, they all felt they could accomplish their goal.

"Alright, alright," Ted continued, "but don't send them to the White House. That's the fastest way for you to draw attention, the wrong kind of attention. Start with the Secretary of the Interior."

The others nodded, hearing Ted's instructions.

"Now," Ted sighed, "can we talk about something boring? Like baseball, maybe? How about some coffee? Who'd like some coffee?"

Martha and Juliana automatically stood and walked together inside David's house to brew. The kids wandered over to the tents to talk. And the adults broke off into various happy conversations. The plan was set. They all knew details could be worked out in the morning.

Chapter 18 - Wait and See

Sue woke up in the arms of David. She didn't care what time it was and hoped she wouldn't hear any sounds from the backyard. All she wanted was to stay right where she was.

David returned the smile and pulled Sue a little closer. He, too, enjoyed the tingle he felt when she was near. He never imagined wanting to settle down with anyone. He didn't think any woman would want to be with an old, crusty curmudgeon like him. But after adopting Zachary and Tyler, his whole outlook changed.

The two lay in bed together and looked in each others' eyes. They didn't need to say anything. They wanted time to freeze.

Unfortunately, with six children sleeping in tents in the backyard on a weekend when friends from all over the country were visiting, there was no way anyone was going to sleep late. The sounds of the boys and the younger girls eventually filtered through the closed bedroom window and into the ears of Sue and

David.

Sue was forced to look at the clock. "Seven-fifteen. I guess that's better than six-thirty."

"Can't we pretend we didn't hear them?"

"Sure," Sue replied. "But you know the others will be awake soon."

"Let's stay here a little longer," David pleaded.

"I wish we could. There's nothing I want more right now. But you know we can't. We have to make coffee and be good hosts."

David knew she was right, but didn't like the idea of getting out of bed. He started to roll over and flip off the sheets, but Sue didn't let go. She smiled at David and squeezed him tight. "Maybe when our guests leave we'll be able to stay in bed a little longer."

"I'd like that. But we'll have a problem."

Sue sat up and looked at him with concern. "What?"

"The boys' room is in my house, the girls' is in yours," David reminded her. "We can't share a room in one house and leave either the girls or the boys alone in the other house."

Sue thought about the problem for a moment, then promptly came up with the solution. "We'll move you and the boys into my house. It's bigger and newer. We can make it even bigger. We'll have to make it bigger. We have to have separate bedrooms for the kids soon because Zachary and Violet will need their own space. We can add rooms on to the house over the porch. I'll talk to Ted."

"I don't think you should," David said.

"Don't you want to?" She asked.

"I definitely would like to share a house," David replied, "but I don't think Ted will pay for additions to your house. Maybe we could wait to add on to the house later and pay for it ourselves. We shouldn't bother Ted."

"Nonsense! Ted's here and we're all excited to be together. This is the perfect time. He'll do it. He likes me," she said and smiled.

"Yes he does," David agreed. "But--"

"C'mon," Sue said, "we gotta get up. Let's go see what the kids are up to."

Reluctantly they got out of bed. Sue brushed her hair while David quickly shaved. They changed their clothes and kissed before leaving the bedroom.

They were shocked to see Denise sitting in the kitchen alone, silent, and nearly asleep. "Are you okay?" Sue asked her.

"Yeah. Bladder."

"Where's your hubbie?" David asked.

"I don't know. He's probably still asleep," Denise replied. "He's learning how to sleep through my morning disruptions."

"But he can't sleep through the kids playing in the backyard," Sue said, pointing outside through the patio door. "Here he comes now. And Juliana's with him."

When Donald and Juliana entered the house, they first greeted Denise.

"Good morning, babe. How are you?" Donald asked.

"See what you two have to look forward to?" Juliana asked Donald and Denise, pointing to the tents in the backyard. "You guys need to have at least one other kid after this one so they can play together at the crack of dawn every day."

"Sorry," Sue apologized.

"Don't be sorry," Juliana told her. "I'm just picking on Denise. You can't expect the kids to be quiet. It's cool."

David handed out mugs of coffee. Shortly after, Janet, Larry and Mary filtered into the kitchen. David handed out more mugs of coffee. And not more than ten minutes later, Patsy, Richard, and Martha opened the patio door screen and entered the kitchen. David handed Martha a mug first, before the others. He remembered that Sue warned him that Martha gets crabby without her first cup in the morning.

Susan and Ted walked into the already-crowded kitchen around 8:00. But as soon as they walked in, Sue kicked them and the others out to have room in the kitchen to cook breakfast. She retained David as her sous chef and server.

Everyone dutifully put on sunscreen after exiting the kitchen. Denise and Juliana made sure the kids were gooped up with SPF-50.

After breakfast in the hot morning sun, the kids all begged to go swimming. Sue approved and they scrambled to the houses to change. The adults relaxed in their chairs to sit in the sun and enjoy the day.

"Well, we know what the kids are going to do today. What are you all going to do?" Ted asked.

"What do you mean, 'you?'" Donald asked.

"I have to leave."

"What?" everyone asked together.

"Yes, sadly, I have appointments first thing tomorrow morning," Ted replied. "Unlike you all, I just can't abandon my responsibilities for four days." He smiled at the others.

"When do you have to leave?" David asked.

"Sometime after lunch. My plane's waiting in

Kansas City. If I get in the air by two or three o'clock, I'll get to where I'm going in time."

"So, Ted, what is it you do when you're not keeping an eye on all of us?" Juliana inquired. "Surely, you have other assignments. Are you allowed to tell us?"

"You remember my Division is responsible for, among other things, determining the origin of intercepted chemical materials. That's why we were called last year; to figure out what the goo was that people found and where it came from." He looked around at the clones and smiled. "Who knew it would lead to you all and eventually lead to this weekend?" He chuckled and shook his head, recalling the highlights of the past year. "But just because I have to monitor all of you doesn't mean I stop doing my other job. So this week I have other potential incidences to attend to. But trust me; nothing is as exciting as following you all." He continued to smile.

"So what are you looking at this week?" Larry asked.

Ted put on his best, official DHS, governmental expression and replied as straight-faced as possible, "I have to go to Wisconsin to look at a herd of cows that are producing lactose-free, fat-free, pasteurized milk right from the udder."

"Really?" Janet asked, surprised.

"Yah, I've heard about 'em, don't ya know. Right from the udder to the refrigerator," Larry added. But he was unable to maintain a straight face. He broke into a sly grin.

"Oh, Lar', you're such a kidder. I almost started believing you," Janet told him.

"You're a little bit too gullible," Mary said to

Janet with a smile. "We need to work on that."

Denise tried to get settled in her chair. Lawn furniture was not designed for pregnant women. She asked Ted, "Have you learned anything else from your friends at the lab since we all left the base?"

"Yes," he answered frankly.

"Can you tell us?" Denise asked eagerly.

"Well, I suppose," Ted replied. "But first you'll all have to take the official oath of secrecy." He looked at Janet to see what response he'd get.

"Secrecy oath?" Janet asked. She thought for a minute and looked at the others, who all sat still, trying not to laugh. "You're kiddin' again, aren't you?"

Everyone broke into laughter. Janet smiled. She didn't mind everyone having a little fun at her expense.

Ted continued, "The lab found out a few things, some interesting things. They tested the mice that transformed at the same time as you all did. It turns out they, too, are sensitive to sunlight. That's why it's so important for you all to continue wearing sunscreen. And it can't hurt the rest us, either," he added looking to Denise and Juliana. "They also found out that the cloned mice can better maintain weight control even if they eat too much or not enough."

"Are you serious? Oh, you're so lucky," Juliana said to Patsy.

"That'd be useful around the holidays," Mary added.

"Larry, you've lost several pounds since last year," Ted acknowledged.

"Yah, I have."

"And you've been eating well, right? Janet's a good cook, correct?"

"You betchya," Larry answered. "She's a great cook, maybe not as good as Sue, but still really good."

"So even after eating well, you've lost weight compared to the original Larry," Ted observed.

"I guess. I'm not sure I remember the other Larry."

"Trust me, you've lost weight," Ted told him. "And that's what the lab found. The cloned mice metabolism is special. It can adjust to maintain weight. You know, it will speed up when too much food is eaten or slow down when the mice don't eat enough."

"And Larry's metabolism obviously corrected his weight. I think Janet may have even lost some pounds, too," Mary added, complimenting Janet.

Janet blushed. "I think you might be right."

"I'm so jealous," Juliana complained.

"Anything else?" Denise asked. "Do they know anything about children of the mice?"

"Ah!" Ted smiled. "Now I know why you asked about the lab. You have a personal interest," Ted said. "In fact, they do know a few things about the second generation."

Everyone sat up in their chairs with interest, especially Denise.

"The mice take after their transformed parent. The lab said the genes from the parent are probably the dominant genes. So the child gets the behavior traits from the transformed parent."

"Oh, sorry hun, you're gonna have a little Donald," Juliana chided.

"I hope he doesn't look like Donald," Patsy added with a smile.

"Hey!" Donald shot back.

"What if it's a girl?" Richard asked, poking fun

at the expecting parents.

"Ew, a little Donaldina!" Juliana cackled. Patsy and Richard laughed along with her, nearly falling off their chairs.

Donald and Denise weren't laughing.

"I'm sorry, Denise," Ted apologized. "Maybe we shouldn't have discussed this so openly."

"It's okay, Ted. *Some* of us are able take this seriously." Denise gave her best friend a sneer. "I'm used to the comments."

"So the baby will have the same metabolism and stuff as Donald?" Sue asked, genuinely interested. "What else will the baby have, Ted?"

"I don't know. What else do you all have?"

"We don't know," Sue replied.

"No one knows yet," Ted responded. "I guess we'll just have to wait and see."

Chapter 19 – That's All

After lunch, Ted stood up and announced it was time for him to leave. The others stood and huddled around him for one last conversation.

"Thank you Sue and David for hosting this weekend. It has been enlightening and entertaining," Ted said. "I'm very glad all of us were able to get together."

Everyone nodded and voiced their agreement.

"Now, before I leave, I need to know what you all plan to do with your letter-writing campaign. I need to know what to expect and what to look out for in Washington."

"We're just going to write letters to the Secretary of the Interior," Patsy said.

"We'll each write letters in our new language and tell the Secretary that there should be more public awareness about the environment," Donald added.

"We'll use the slogan that Patsy came up with," Sue said.

"You'll need to provide a key to deciphering the

language, so the Secretary can actually read the letters," David told the clones.

"And then maybe we'll send letters to the White House to get the President's wife and daughters to help," Brandy suggested.

"All of that sounds good, except for the First Family. Sorry Brandy," Ted apologized. "Just write to the Secretary of the Interior for now."

He turned and looked each of the clones in the eyes, even the children, before continuing. "Promise me you won't do anything crazy. Promise me all you will do is write letters. Nothing else. No visits," he added, looking at Sue. "No road trips in your car," he said to Larry. "No college protests or rallies," he said to Patsy and Martha. "And no using your job inside the department," he said to Donald. "Just write letters."

"Don't you trust us?" Sue asked.

"Yes..." he paused. "Yes, I do trust you, but I have to make sure things don't get out of hand. This needs to stay simple."

"We hear your words, Ted," Mary began speaking, "but I don't feel your sincerity. I don't think you *do* trust them."

"I do. I really do. But..."

"Ted," Sue told him, walking up and placing her hand on his arm, "we'll just write letters. There will be nothing to worry about."

"That's what I'm worried about. We all think there will be nothing to worry about, but then there's always something that we'll have to worry about."

"It's just letters, Ted. And all they'll suggest is to clean up the planet. That's all," David insisted.

"Promise me that's all you'll do," Ted said to everyone.

In unison, they all replied, "We promise."

"Alright. Good."

Everyone smiled with each other over Ted's acceptance of the plan.

"Now I'm afraid I must be going. Thanks again to everyone for your hospitality, friendship and engaging conversation. This has truly been a unique weekend."

When he started to walk to his car, he pulled Mary aside and quietly asked, "Will you please keep an eye on them and their letters? If I'm going to hear about this from the Department, I want to know about it before."

"I will, Ted. Take care."

Ted waved to all, turned, and walked around the house.

"Oh wait!" Sue exclaimed. She ran around the house after Ted. A few minutes later she returned.

The others looked at her, confused, asking for an explanation.

"Nothing," she replied. "I just had something to ask Ted. It's nothing important," she told them with wave of her hand. "Now, what should we write in our letters?"

Chapter 20 – Top Priority

When he turned onto I-70, Ted dialed Jim Bailey on his phone.

"Jim. It's Ted. ... Nope, nothing's wrong. ... I learned something this weekend. Actually, I learned a lot this weekend. I told you on Friday that our friends can all read and write the same language that Sue could earlier this year. The others only realized it when they got here to Kansas. That proves my theory about proximity. It takes at least four or five of the clones together to get a message. Without that many, they can't receive a message. ... Yeah, there's more. The clones believe that the messages they've received about the new language this year and the dead planet and extinct species last year were meant for them. They think they're supposed to deliver those messages. They're going to start a letter-writing campaign. ... Yeah, you think it's a good idea now, Jim, but just wait. These things always turn out differently than planned. I don't know what's going to happen here, but I've got to be ready for anything. ... I need you to give your mice the million-dollar work-up. I need to know everything about these mice. What they can do, what extra behavior they have, what advantageous traits they have, everything. Make this your top priority. ... Call me as soon as you get the results. I need to know what these clones can do. ... I don't know if they'll do anything crazy. I don't think so. But if they get more messages, I'm not sure what will happen. ... Thanks Jim. I'll be in touch."

Ted hung up the phone and continued his drive to Kansas City.

Chapter 21 – We're Ready

After dinner, everyone sat in the backyard around the fire, even the kids.

"Sue, David, this has been a great weekend together," Juliana called out. "Thank you so much for hosting all of us."

All the others voiced their agreement.

"It's a shame we have to leave tomorrow," Martha added. "I wish we could stay longer."

"I wish you all could stay longer," Sue replied with regret, "but we have our other lives to go back to."

"Not 'other lives,'" Patsy responded cheerfully. "We have one life, just different parts. Martha and I have Cupz. I have Richard and school. And I have you all. So we aren't stopping one life to go to the other, we're just moving from one part to the other. But now we're not really separating one part from another because we're going to write our letters back home. So we're bringing this part to our home part."

"Nicely put," Mary commended.

"So what are we going to write in our letters?"

Brandy asked.

"We need to convince the Secretary of the Interior to start a campaign to get people to clean up the planet," Donald said.

"We should each say something about the planet and how we don't want it to become dead like the other," Brandy said.

"Might I make a suggestion?" Mary asked the group. "I think you need more than just opinions and desires. Don't get me wrong, all of your ideas, especially written in your language, will be considerably effective. But I think you will also need to collect data from the internet to help substantiate your claims."

"What do you mean?" Brandy asked.

"Find facts about the environment, global warming, the ozone layer, the polar ice cap, and the oceans. Find actual data from reputable scientists and include those in your letters. That way, the Secretary will read your personal beliefs, but will also have data."

"Do you think we can find a lot of stuff about the environment on the internet?" Sue asked.

"Absolutely," Mary replied. "You just have to find accurate data from real scientists. There's a lot of incorrect information out there."

"Okay. We should all go home and do some research. Then we can write letters in our language and send them," Sue proposed.

"What about the key that you mentioned, David?" Patsy asked.

"If you're writing in a foreign language or code," David began, "you have to provide your reader with a key to break the code so they can translate into English. Let me get some paper to explain." David went inside, turning the outdoor lights on as he did.

He quickly returned with paper and pencils and sat at a table while the others crowded around. "If you wrote everything in numbers where one equals the letter a, and two equals b, and three equals c, and so on, the word 'cab' would be written as three-one-two. See? Now that's pretty simple, but if you start writing really complicated things it's going to get messy. So the key to the code would be included in the message. You would write one equals a, two equals b, and so on."

"So we need to write the letters of our language and then tell the Secretary what letters these are in English," Brandy said.

Richard, who had been quiet for a long time, jumped into the conversation, "Why don't you make it a little more challenging. Why don't you include a sentence or phrase to translate from your language to English." He looked around to see if the others were following his suggestion. "What phrase do we know that would be perfect for this?"

The clones were thinking but couldn't readily come up with the answer.

"Donald? Do you know of a phrase that might work?" Richard asked, leading Donald. "Something from your typing class, maybe?"

"Oh! The quick brown fox jumps over the lazy dog! Yeah, that'll be great!"

The others agreed with Richard's suggestion.

"We'll put 'The quick brown fox jumps over the lazy dog' in our language on every letter we write," Donald told the others.

"Let's practice," Brandy said.

"Conveniently, I have a lot of paper and pencils," David noted.

The clones all took seats at the table writing in

their language. The adults were able to master the writing quickly, but the children had a little trouble.

Martha said to the others, "Don't forget Patsy's slogan. What was it again?"

Brandy replied, "You live on this planet. Clean up after yourself!"

"Yeah, that's it. Don't forget to practice that, too," Martha instructed the group.

After twenty more minutes of practicing, Sue looked over the others' papers, especially the kids' papers, and said to all, "I think we got it. We're ready to send our letters."

Chapter 22 - Goodbye

Sue woke up in David's arms. *Three days in a row!* She snuggled up against him and closed her eyes with a smile. The only sounds she could hear were David's soft breathing and birds chirping outside. *My own little birdies must still be sleeping*, she thought. *Either that or it's only 5:30.* She looked at the clock: 7:00. She nuzzled even closer to David. She wished it actually was 5:30 so she could have at least another hour in his arms. But she knew it wouldn't happen.

She and David were able to hold each other for another ten minutes before the sounds of people stirring wafted into the bedroom through the window screen.

Sue heard the patio door slide open, followed by the kids starting to talk and giggle in the yard. David woke and squeezed her tight.

"C'mon," Sue reluctantly said. "We gotta get up." She sat up and tried to straighten her hair. "I bet Denise is in the kitchen waiting for coffee."

"I don't want to," David protested, whining like

Tyler.

"You don't have a choice. Get up," she playfully responded with a slap to his butt.

The two slowly stood up and made themselves somewhat presentable. Sue put on David's sweatpants and untwisted her night shirt. David put on a t-shirt and slipped shorts over his boxers. They hugged and kissed one last time before exiting to the kitchen.

As they guessed, Denise was in the kitchen. She had started a pot of coffee and was sitting at the table reading the newspaper. "Good morning," she whispered when she saw Sue and David.

"Good morning," Sue whispered back. "How are you today?"

"So far, so good. But I do have to sit on a plane today to fly back to California. At least I'm not yet too big to fit in the seats, so I won't be too uncomfortable. Boy, I'd hate to fly if I was in my third trimester."

"What does it feel like being pregnant?" Sue asked.

"Don't get any ideas," warned David.

"Well, you feel full all the time," Denise replied, "but you're hungry all the time too. And the baby kicks. And it sits on your bladder so you have to pee a lot. And you can't walk very well. You start to lean back when you walk to balance the weight. And the hormone surges are a real pain in the ass."

"That doesn't sound enjoyable at all," Sue responded.

"Good answer," David said. "No fun at all."

Denise turned to Sue with a smile on her face. "It's the most wonderful feeling in the world."

"Damn," David sighed.

"Oh David, don't worry," Sue told him. "We aren't even married yet. I can't have a baby without first being married."

"Oh great," David said to Denise. "Now she's talking marriage. I'm not sure this bedroom-sharing thing was such a good idea." He shook his head. "What have I gotten into?"

"Your new life," Denise replied with a big smile.

Sue also gave David a big smile.

The children came inside the house asking what was for breakfast. After quieting them down a little, Sue served orange juice while David made bowls of cereal.

"Do you have any coffee?" Brandy asked.

Denise looked at her with shock. "Coffee?"

"Ew!" Karen replied.

"Yeah, ew!" Kati added.

"You guys drink a lot of coffee, so I thought I'd try it," Brandy responded. "Actually, Katelyn's mom makes us lattes sometimes," she admitted.

"Well this is caffeinated, so only a half a cup at most. I don't need you bouncing off the walls in the plane later."

"Uh, Mom," she replied. "Hello? Soda? It's got caffeine in it. So like, I've been having caffeine for a long time. No need to worry about one cup of coffee."

"You're right, you're right. My bad," Denise said. "Load her up, Sue."

As David brought cereal to the younger kids, he poked fun at Brandy, "Would you like some oatmeal, or maybe some raisin bran, or maybe some granola cereal now that you're so old?"

"No, I can still have some Lucky Charms."

"Lucky Charms and coffee," David said, shaking his head. "*Eeeew*," he added, mocking the girls.

Larry and Janet filtered into the kitchen followed shortly by Mary. The rest of the group soon arrived from Sue's house. David had the second pot of coffee brewing when they walked in the kitchen. He got a cup for Martha first.

After the caffeine kicked in, Sue asked, "When do you all have to leave? Not that I want you to go, but I want to make sure you're all on time.

Juliana, who made the reservations, responded, "The van leaves at nine-thirty to go to Kansas City. The Wisconsin car can leave a half hour later. Or we can all leave at once if that's easier. Our flights are all around twelve-thirty to one o'clock."

"We don't have much time then," Mary replied. "Is everybody packed?"

"No way," Donald exclaimed. "I've got a lot of packing to do."

"Not much for us," Patsy replied.

"We're packed already," Janet said.

"Let's have a quick breakfast," David suggested, "then the rest of you can go pack."

They all agreed. Juliana and Donald sat inside with Denise and the kids. The others took their coffee and sat outside.

Sue and David made several batches of scrambled eggs and toast for the adults. They served Denise and Donald first so the pregnant Denise could eat and Donald could go pack. The adults outdoors were served next. Sue and David ate last.

After breakfast, the kids played in the yard while the adult travelers went to their respective rooms to pack. By 9:00, everyone had assembled at the tables in the backyard, suitcases by their sides.

"Thank you so much for coming here to visit. This has been the best weekend ever," Sue told all.

"Thanks for having us," Patsy replied. "We've all had a lot of fun."

The others nodded and voiced agreement.

"So we all know what we're going to do when we get home, right?" Sue asked.

"Yeah, we're all going to look up data and write letters in our language to send to the Secretary of the Interior. Pretty simple," Brandy replied.

"Do we need to review the letters with each other before we send them?" Janet asked.

"That's a good point," Patsy responded. "We should probably send what we're going to write so our letters are similar. We need to write the same kind of stuff so we sound like we're all together."

"Okay, let's plan to do that," Donald told all.

"We can reply to all if we think the writer should make a change," Sue added.

"Be careful," Mary warned. "You could spend a lot of time editing and re-editing text if all of you keep sending letters back and forth between you. You should only suggest changes if there are big differences. Otherwise, just share the letters for information."

"That's also a good point," Patsy said. "Okay, we'll only send emails for information, so we can see what each other is writing. And only if there's a big problem will we reply. How's that sound?"

The others agreed.

"Hey, are we gonna get to write letters too?" Zachary asked.

"Sure, you guys can definitely write letters,"

Patsy said, looking at the children. "I'm sure Sue can help you."

"I can," Sue confirmed.

"Cool!" Tyler exclaimed.

Juliana called out, "I think we should get the cars loaded. I'm guessing it will take a while to say goodbye." She paused and smiled. "Also, Denise will need the time to waddle out front."

Denise was just close enough to slug her friend in the arm.

Everyone stood up and began the walk to the front, carrying their suitcases and overnight bags. When they reached the van and rental car, they loaded the bags in the back.

Sue started the hugging to say goodbye, and everyone else joined in. Ten minutes later, after each had made departing comments to each other, the travelers got in their vehicles.

Sue, David, and the Kansas kids walked to the end of the driveway as the car and van backed out. They waved continually until the vehicles disappeared around the corner.

The long weekend was over.

Chapter 23 - Five

The rest of the week passed as usual, except Sue only had to work four days instead of five. On Saturday she woke up in her bed, alone. She wished that she was in David's arms, but it wasn't to be. They hadn't yet figured out how to move the boys over to the new house. David didn't want to displace them from real beds and Sue agreed it wasn't fair to the boys. But she missed that special feeling she had waking up with David.

She slowly got out of bed and went downstairs to make coffee. Kati and Violet were quietly watching TV in the family room off the kitchen.

"Good morning, ladies."

"Hi Mommy!" Kati replied.

"Hi Mom," Violet added cheerfully.

"Are you two ready to write some letters today?" Sue asked.

"As long as we can play and swim too," Kati answered. "I don't want to spend the whole day doing boring stuff."

"It's not boring, Kati," Violet corrected. "It's good for the environment. We need to help the environment. Brandy told me," she added.

"Okay, but I still want to swim."

"You can certainly go swimming," Sue reassured her. "Now, should we have breakfast here first and then go wake up the boys, or should we go wake them up now?"

"Let's go wake 'em up now!" Kati happily replied.

But they didn't need to. After a quick knock, the door opened. Tyler and Zachary burst through, followed by David. "Good morning," David said to Sue.

"Good morning," she replied, moving close to him for a hug and a kiss. "Coffee?"

"I'd like that," he said, holding her tight.

"You'll have to let me go."

"The coffee can wait another minute."

But the children could not. "Can we have cereal and toast, Mommy?" Kati interrupted.

"Sure. Why don't you all sit at the table and I'll start toasting. Would you be so kind as to pour juice?" she asked David.

"My pleasure," he replied.

During breakfast Sue started talking about the letters they were going to write. She said she had to check email to see if any of the others had sent ideas or copies of the letters they had written. After that, they could do some research on the internet to see what they wanted to include in the letters.

"Research? Is that like homework?" Zachary complained. "It's summer."

"A little research won't kill you," David

responded. "You want to be part of the letters that we're all writing, don't you?"

"Yeah, but you can do the research," Zachary said, looking to Sue and David. "We'll just help you write the words."

"You can't get off that easy, young man. And neither can the rest of you," David informed the other children.

The kids were temporarily dismissed to go outside while David cleaned up the kitchen and Sue retrieved her laptop. She sat at the counter and read her email. The oldest unread message was from Brandy, sent on Thursday night.

"Here's a message from Brandy," Sue said to David. "Let's see... back in Burbank... it's hot... got some ideas... tried to write them out... David, come read this! Look! Brandy and Donald tried to write a letter in the new language, but they couldn't. They tried for a long time, but they couldn't make any of the letters. What does that mean?"

"I don't know," David replied. He sat next to Sue and thought. After a moment, he replied, "Ted said he thought the new language was triggered by all of you being together. But that was the trigger. Once you know something, you should be able to do it at any time. It's like riding a bike. But if they can't write it when they're back in California..."

"They must have just forgotten. I'll tell them to practice more when I reply to their email," Sue calmly said. "Let's look at these other messages. Here's one from Patsy." She clicked on the message and started reading. "Hot in Arizona... coffee shop... tried to write letters... Same thing!" she called out. "They couldn't write the new language either."

"You better see if you have a message from Janet or Larry," David suggested.

"Right." She scanned her inbox and found the message from Janet. "Here it is. Janet sent the message to everyone. She says that they tried to write in the language but they couldn't. She's asking if the others had the same trouble."

"Did Patsy or Brandy reply?"

"Let me check. Uh…yeah, Brandy replied to all saying that she and Donald couldn't either."

"Is there a message from Patsy?"

"Um… Yeah. She thinks that we have to be together." Sue looked at David and asked, "Do you think we all have to be together?"

"You and the kids could write the language. That wasn't all of you. The others, they only have two clones in one place. We have five."

Sue stood and walked to the front door. "Kids!" she called outside. "Please come inside. We need to test something."

They made their way toward the house, still tossing the ball as they walked. When they got inside, Sue told them to stand by her at the counter. David brought in paper and pencils.

"We need to do some test writing in our language to see if we remember it," Sue told them. "What should I write?"

"How about 'the quick brown fox?'" Violet replied.

"Good idea," Sue said. She started carefully writing on the paper and the same swirled, geometric text emerged from her pencil, just as it had a couple months ago. "Can you read this?" she asked. "Zachary, what does this say?"

"The quick brown fox jumped over the lazy dog. That's what you said you'd write," he replied.

"David, can you read this?"

"Nope."

"So that's what it is," Sue concluded. "There have to be more than two people together to write the letters."

"What's goin' on?" Tyler asked, confused.

"The others cannot write in our language now that they are back at their homes. They tried, but they can't. Brandy and Donald tried, Patsy and Martha tried, and Janet and Larry tried. But none of them could. So I wanted to see if we still could. And we can," Sue said.

"What does that mean?" Violet asked. "What do we do?"

"It means that you five get to write all the letters," David replied.

Sue briefly thought about the meaning and then decided there was no alternative. "I better reply to everyone and tell them what we found out. I hope that they will still send their ideas to me so I can write them in our language," Sue said. "I don't want to write up all these ideas by myself."

"We'll help," Violet told Sue.

"Yeah, we can write too," Kati added.

"Yes, but we need ideas from everybody so that it's not only our ideas. We'll get ideas from the others, and then we'll actually write the letters. How's that sound?"

"Good," Violet replied.

The other children agreed.

"Okay, you all can go out and play. I need to send an email to everyone. Go on. We'll write letters later."

The children took their ball and went back outside to resume their game.

"Do you want any assistance?" David asked.

"Sure, you can help me look stuff up on the internet," Sue replied. "You'll have to stay close to me so we can both see the screen," she added with a grin. "I hope you don't mind."

"Aw, do I have to?" David whined sarcastically.

Sue pulled a stool next to her and David sat at the kitchen counter close to her. She typed an email to the others asking them to send draft letters to her by email so she could then write them on paper. David put his arm around Sue's waist and quietly watched.

"There. I hope we get some letter ideas soon."

"You probably will," David responded. "If the others were trying to write letters in the new language, they probably already had ideas. I bet you'll get emails back today."

"I hope so. Now, how do we look up stuff about the environment? What do we start with?"

"You'll have to start with real data. A lot of people have a lot of opinions about the environment. But opinions don't matter," he told her. "Data is what's important."

Sue looked at him with confusion.

"Most of the problem with believing or not believing that global warming is a problem is that people only hear or read opinions," David told her. "Those that don't believe global warming is happening try to say that that there's no proof and it's just a phase. And scientists say otherwise and try to present real data. But the naysayers claim they can't collect enough data to actually *prove* it. Then everyone just goes back and forth arguing with each other and no one gets anywhere."

"So I need experts," Sue concluded. "But if I don't know who the experts are, how do I look them up?"

"Search on Google for global warming experts and see what you get."

She did. When the results came back, she said, "All of these links talk about experts in general, like there's a group of these people that travel together and everyone calls them the experts. But there are hardly any names here. It's just groups."

"Look. One of these links is a list of experts from a group. Open it up," David suggested.

Sue clicked the link. When the document opened she responded, "There are six people on this list. That's it? There are only six experts in the world?"

"No. There are six people on this list," David replied with a laugh. "Whoever made this list was recording the contact information for these people, you know, websites, phone numbers and stuff. So this is not the complete list. It was probably a list of speakers at a conference or something. It's a small list of experts, but, it's a place to start. Google the first guy on the list."

Sue did. "Hey! This guy is a professor at Berkley. What's Berkley?"

"It's a really good university in California. It's near San Francisco."

"So this guy is a teacher. If he teaches, he must be an expert. What do all these links point to?" Sue asked.

"Click on them and see where they take you."

Sue began clicking and reading. Soon she became absorbed in her research. Her clicking and reading took her deeper into her subject. After twenty minutes, she barely heard David speak.

"I need to go mow the lawn. I'll put the kids in the pool," he said.

"Yeah, okay," Sue absent-mindedly replied, her eyes glued to the computer screen.

Three hours later, when David returned from outside, Sue was still clicking and reading. "Would you like some lunch?" David asked. "The kids and I are hungry. Can I make you something?"

"Lunch?" Sue asked, finally breaking her eyes away from the computer. "We just ate breakfast."

"Yeah, four hours ago," David told her. "I've mowed the lawn, and the kids have been playing in the pool all morning. I even took a swim with them."

"Have I been here for four hours?"

"Yep."

"Wow. That long?" she asked. David nodded. "I found a lot of cool stuff!" she said excitedly. "I found a reporter who's written a whole bunch of stuff about climate change. And the reviews say it's really good writing because she's not a scientist and she's not a politician. So she can look at the results ob... ob--"

"Objectively."

"Yeah, that's it. And she doesn't talk about the results like a politician, the reviews said. Why do politicians not think global warming is a problem? Why don't they want to fix the environment?"

"I'm not sure," David replied. "If I had to guess, I'd say it's because it will cost a lot of money."

"Huh?"

"To deal with all the pollution means we have to change. And changing costs money," David told her. "We have to do something different than what is causing the problem. We have to burn less coal to make electricity, and we have to drive less or make cars with better gas mileage, and we have to develop alternative energies. All this costs money. The government can either force the energy and car companies to pay for all of this, or the government can pay for these things. Either way, someone has to pay."

"So why don't the companies pay?" Sue asked.

"If they have to pay more to fix the problem, they'll make less profit," David replied. "If they make less profit, they may go out of business. So, companies don't want to pay to fix the environment. And companies tell politicians that."

"Why do the politicians listen? Why don't they just tell the companies to pay?"

"Because companies give them money," David told her.

"Huh?"

"Companies give money to certain politicians' campaigns to get those certain politicians elected. Then the politicians pass laws that help the companies make more profit."

"That's not right," Sue protested.

"That's politics here in America," David replied.

"So then let the companies raise prices instead of losing money," Sue suggested.

"If they raise prices, all of us citizens will have to pay more to get our electricity or to drive a car."

"I'm okay with that," Sue replied.

"Yes, but you aren't like most people," David told her. "Most people do not want to pay more. Some people *can't* pay more. And people don't think it's up to them to pay to fix the environment."

"But they live on this planet," Sue argued. "So

'Clean up after yourself!' That's what we're writing about."

"Exactly. But it's a very difficult message to try to deliver. Most citizens are happy as long as someone else pays," David replied.

"So then the government can pay," Sue declared. "Politicians must pass laws to force the government to pay."

"Where does the government get money?" David asked her.

Sue looked at him confused.

"Taxes," he replied. "And who pays taxes?"

"We all do."

"Exactly. And do we all like to pay taxes?"

"I don't know. I thought we had to," she said.

"Do you want to pay even more taxes?"

"To fix the environment? Sure, I'll pay more taxes," she replied.

"Yes, but most people don't agree with you," David responded. "Most people hate to pay taxes and don't want to pay any more. So the politicians become very unpopular when they suggest raising taxes."

"So?"

"So when they are unpopular…" He tried leading her to the conclusion.

Sue responded with more confusion, shaking her head.

"They don't get re-elected," David told her. "And that's what politicians fear worse than death: not being re-elected."

"So because it will eventually cost companies or citizens more money to fix the environment, and companies pay for politicians' elections, and citizens elect politicians, the politicians are scared to pass laws to fix the environment," Sue summarized. "Because if citizens have to pay more money, we'll be mad and then we won't re-elect the politicians."

"Exactly."

"I don't get it," Sue declared, shaking her head.

"What don't you get?" David asked.

"Just because some guys in the government want to keep their jobs, the environment won't get fixed?"

"The environment won't get fixed by politicians," David told her. "It's up to the people to make the changes for the good of the environment."

"So?"

"So that's what you all are doing with your letters," David informed her. "Your letters are suggesting a slogan to convince the people of this country that saving the planet is everyone's responsibility."

"I hope our letters work."

Chapter 24 - Letters

Sue looked in her email inbox. Overnight, she received messages from Brandy, Patsy, and Janet. Per Sue's suggestion, each of them had sent their ideas for letters.

"Let's see what Brandy wrote," Sue said to David. The two were sitting in Sue's family room, avoiding the rain and thunder that was passing through Kansas. David read his book while Sue read Brandy's email out loud.

"Hey Sue," she began, "I got an idea for a letter to write. D and D helped a little. Kids don't like being lectured by adults about what's right and what to do. And adults are sometimes not even in touch with what's going on. They don't know how to communicate with us. So my letter is going tell the Secretary how to get in touch with kids. If anyone is going do something to fix the environment, it's going be kids."

"She's right about that," David responded. "Adults sure aren't gonna fix the environment. Not at the rate things are going now."

"Here's her letter. Do you want me to read it to you?" she asked.

"Yes, please," he answered.

"Dear Mr. Secretary. It's obvious that global warming is a problem. There's so much data that it can't be denied. So everyone on the planet has got to do something about it. We all have to do our part. Teens in America are ready to help the environment, Mr. Secretary, but we need to work together. So we need to be connected. And the best way to connect is to use social media like Facebook, Twitter, YouTube, and Instagram. If the Department of the Interior would post ideas for real changes that people can do to fix the environment, the ideas will spread. We don't want to see articles and news reports. We want to see real ideas. Teens will communicate with each other and the ideas will go viral. I also suggest a new phrase for you to use when posting ideas online: You live on this planet, so clean up after yourself! Thank you, sincerely, Brandy Jackson."

"Sounds like Brandy has a good idea for what the department can do," David commented. "What do you think?"

"I like it!" Sue replied. "But I don't know a lot about Facebook or Twitter."

"That's because you're old," he said.

"I'm not that old!"

"Yeah, but you're not thirteen, and not in junior high or high school."

"Do you think her idea will work? Will the ideas spread?" Sue asked.

"I don't know," David answered. "I guess we have to trust Brandy. She's pretty smart and is more in touch with teenagers than we are. So, yeah, I think it will work. Or at least it's worth sending her letter."

"I agree," Sue replied. "Should I read Patsy's email to you?"

"Sure."

"Hi Sue. I'm sending you my letter. Richard and Martha helped me write it. I decided to focus on our message and not a lot on trying to convince the Secretary that global warming is a problem. I'm assuming that he already knows.

"Do you think that's correct?" Sue asked David. "Do you think that the Secretary already knows?"

"Yes," David replied. "But has he accepted it? Is he willing to fix it? We don't know."

Sue continued reading Patsy's email. "Mr. Secretary, it is obvious to the general community that the environment is a mess. By that, I mean that polar ice caps are melting, the global surface temperature is rising, ocean currents are fluctuating, and air quality is deteriorating. All of these are caused by pollution issued by factories, power plants and automobiles. Just like a family who lives in a house where messes happen and must clean up after themselves, the residents of our house, Planet Earth, must do a little cleaning. By that I mean we have to reduce emissions that cause global warming. We need to use less electricity so we don't have to burn as much coal at power plants. We need to find alternative sources to generate electricity. We need to make factories more efficient. And we need more public transportation in our largest cities. But you and citizens of this country know that. What we are missing is a slogan that you and the government can use to promote reducing emissions by emphasizing we are all residents in the same house. We have that slogan: You live on this planet. Clean up after yourself! Please consider using this slogan in a promotional campaign. It's important."

"Richard was right," David commented. "She *is* good. She should go into advertising when she gets her degree."

"That was a really good letter," Sue concluded. "I'll read Janet's now, okay? Ready?"

"Yep."

"Hi Sue. I wrote this letter. Larry dictated a lot to me. And Mary helped too. We wanted to keep the letter simple. Here it is. To Mr. Secretary, please consider our request to start a new awareness campaign to alert citizens of this great country about what can be done to fix the environment. There is no doubt that something needs to be done. Like most other citizens in the U.S., we want to help clean the environment. The problem is that we do not have a leader. People of the United States look to the government at times like these. We are all looking to you now. We suggest that the Department of the Interior start an awareness campaign for people to follow. We suggest: You live on this planet, clean up after yourself! If you use this slogan in your awareness campaign, we're sure people of the US will follow your lead. Thank you."

"That's another good letter," David said. "And each one is different from the others. So what are *you* going to write?"

"I think we need to include some expert's quotes," Sue declared. "I think we need to reinforce that experts say that the environment is a problem. I want to use quotes by that reporter that I found yesterday. Do you think that's a good idea?"

"The others didn't include any data in their

letters," David replied. "And I don't think they need to. Like Patsy said, the Secretary already knows about the data. But it can't hurt to include quotes from a reporter. It reinforces that people in the media are writing about the environment. Politicians pay attention to what the media says. So yeah, I think you should include it."

"Okay, I will," Sue said. "I have to look up the quotes again."

David returned to reading his book while Sue searched the internet. After finding the articles she was looking for, she started typing her letter.

After 30 minutes of silence, Sue finally spoke. "Do you want to hear my letter?"

"Absolutely," David replied.

"Okay, here goes. Dear Mr. Secretary. There seems to be no doubt that global warming is a problem. Scientists have the data. People know about the data. And reporters write about the data. For example, Elizabeth Kolbert wrote, 'As best as can be determined, the world is now warmer than it has been at any point in the last two millennia, and, if current trends continue, by the end of the century it will likely be hotter than at any point in the last two million years.' She also wrote, 'In the same way that global warming has gradually ceased to be merely a theory, so, too, its impacts are no longer just hypothetical.' And she wrote, 'It may seem impossible to imagine that a technologically advanced society could choose, in essence, to destroy itself, but that is what we are now in the process of doing.' Mr. Secretary, this country needs to lead the effort around the world to fix the environment. You can be the leader. I suggest you start with the slogan that my friends have also suggested: You live on this planet.

Clean up after yourself! If you can deliver this message, people of the United States and reporters around the world will write about the good things you are doing to clean the environment. Thank you Mr. Secretary."

"As always, Sue, you get right to the point," David said with a smile. "I can always count on you to tell it like it is."

"Is it a good letter?"

"It's good," David told her. "Now all you and the kids have to do is write these up."

"Good thing it's raining," she said. She called upstairs to the kids. They slowly came down the stairs, the boys leading the way.

"You've been awfully quiet," David noted as they filtered into the family room. "What have you been doing?"

"Sleeping," Zachary responded. "I'm bored."

"I was reading," Violet proudly announced.

"Yeah, reading a magazine," Tyler informed Sue. "One of those dumb pink girl magazines," he added.

"You're such a dork," Violet shot back.

"Yeah," Kati echoed. "You're such a dork."

"Okay, okay. That's enough," Sue told the kids, breaking up the spat. "It's time to write some letters. Are you ready?"

"I guess so," Tyler replied.

The others reluctantly agreed.

"Good. Let's get started."

By dinner time, the four letters had been transcribed into the clone's language. Sue supervised the children who actually wrote the letters. They only needed a few do-overs because of mistakes. David reminded Sue to include the 'quick brown fox' key at the bottom of each letter. After proof-reading each one, she put the letters into their own envelopes and sealed them. She found the mailing address online, wrote it on the envelopes, included her return address, and stamped them.

"I'll mail these tomorrow before work," Sue told David. "I wonder how long we'll have to wait before we get a response."

Chapter 25 – The Key

Ted took his seat in front of the committee. He was tired after having to wake early to travel to Washington, D.C. He had been summoned the night before for the urgent meeting at 9:00 a.m. the next day. He drank coffee, restlessly shifted his body in the chair, and braced himself for the questions.

"What the hell is going on, Ted?" the general bellowed.

"Um, I'm not sure," Ted quietly replied. "Can you please enlighten me?"

"These letters!" the chairman exclaimed as he pointed to Mr. Mason.

Mr. Mason dutifully held up the envelopes and letters sent by Sue.

"The FBI intercepted these a few days ago and brought them to us," the general told Ted.

"I don't know if I can say for sure what is going on," Ted replied. He was evading the question so he wouldn't have to implicate himself in the letter-writing campaign his friends started.

"Dammit! Your people started writing letters to the Secretary of the Interior!"

"My people?"

"The aliens, Ted! We have the return address right here on the envelope. It's the one in Kansas, the one who escaped the base last year! What the hell is she doing? Aren't you keeping an eye on these people?"

"I am. But I cannot control every action."

"She wrote to the Secretary in some sort of scribbled language... swirls and shapes and stuff. It looks like freakin' hieroglyphics! What the hell does this mean?"

Ted squirmed even more in his chair. General Gilmore was making him just as uncomfortable as his suit. "The clones are apparently writing the Secretary."

"Really. We couldn't figure *that* out," Mr. Wright sarcastically replied. "What do they want?"

"I'm not sure. What did they write?"

"We can't read the damn things, Ted!" the general barked. "Dammit! You know more than you're telling us. Don't jerk us around. Answer us."

"I don't know what they wrote. I can't read the language either. Did the FBI get anything out of the writing?"

"They tried, but couldn't get anything," Mr. Mason replied.

Ted smiled. He knew the FBI wasn't as smart as the rest of the department thought. He sat up straight in his chair and smugly asked the committee members, "Did you look for a key?"

"A key?" the general asked.

"A key, you know, to decipher the message. This is Intelligence 101, guys," Ted replied.

"The FBI couldn't find anything. The only common writing included on each one of the letters was this one bit here," Mr. Mason pointed out as he held up one of the letters.

"And?" Ted asked.

"Nothing conclusive," Mr. Mason replied.

"They think it might be the group's name," Mr. Wright added. "You know, like a terrorist group claiming responsibility."

"What did they write, Ted?" the general hollered. "Tell us!"

Like I said, I don't know. I can't read what they wrote." Ted waited to see how the committee would react. He liked making them squirm a little too, which they did. Finally, he told them, "But they *did* give you the key."

"Huh?" the general asked, confused.

"The one line of text that's written on each letter, General, is a key."

"Tell us," the general instructed.

"The quick brown fox jumps over the lazy dog."

"What?"

"I don't know for sure," Ted said, "but if I'm correct, the key is 'the quick brown fox jumps over the lazy dog.'"

"Huh?" the general responded, even more confused than before.

"Didn't you ever take a typing course?" Ted asked, looking at the three committee members. "The phrase contains every letter of the alphabet. It teaches you how to find all the keys on the keyboard."

The committee stared at him with confusion.

Ted rolled his eyes in frustration. "That phrase

tells you which letter of the alphabet corresponds to each symbol of their language."

"Oh," the general responded. He turned to his aide and instructed, "Make a note of that. And contact the FBI."

Ted sat back in his chair and shook his head in disbelief. He wondered how these men could be so clueless.

"So if *you* know the key, what do the messages say?" Mr. Wright asked. "Surrender the planet?"

"Um, it's probably more like 'clean the planet.'"

"What?" Mr. Mason asked.

"They sent the letters to the Secretary of the Interior. If it was an ultimatum to surrender the planet, they would have sent it to the Department of Defense or the President. These are letters are about the environment. If you recall, they received a message last year from an extinct species from a dead planet. Remember? That was kind of the whole point of sending the goo, right? The extinct species sent the substance to other planets as a memory of their species and to warn the people on other planets not to allow the same extinction to occur. The residents here on Earth, who were cloned from the goo, don't want to end up extinct like that species. These people are trying to save themselves and everyone else on the planet."

The committee sat in silence trying to digest what Ted told them.

Realizing it would take a very long time for them to understand, Ted asked the men, "Can I go now?"

Chapter 26 – Independence Day

Sue came skidding into the garage on her bike. She hopped off and dropped it. She ran through the yard, saying "Hello" to David and the kids without stopping.

When she exited her house ten minutes later, she was clean, dressed in shorts and a t-shirt, and walked calmly with a smile. "I'm *so* glad to be done working," Sue said when she sat in a chair on David's patio. "I had fun today," she told him. "The crowd was great. But now it's time for us to celebrate. What time are the fireworks?"

"They'll start around 9:30," David replied.

"Oh, that's too bad," Sue said loudly with a straight face. "Some little ones will have to miss the firewoks since they'll all be in bed."

The four kids immediately objected.

"Hey!"

"No Way!"

"Uh uh!"

"That's not fair!"

Sue didn't break her serious expression. "That's just too late for you four to stay up. I'm sorry."

"But it's our first Fourth of July!" Violet protested.

"Yeah, we've never seen the fireworks before!" Kati added. "It's not fair!"

"Dad!" Zachary appealed to David. "C'mon… let us stay up. It'll only be like 10:00 and we promise we'll go right to bed."

"I don't know, I think I agree with Sue," David replied, trying to look serious. "That's awfully late."

Sue let the kids simmer for a few seconds before breaking into a smile. "Just kidding! Of course you can stay up! We've got a whole night of fun planned!"

The children burst into excitement, running and jumping in the yard.

"Why don't you all get your suits on and go swimming," David suggested.

The kids readily agreed and scrambled to their respective rooms to get changed.

"I do want to check email and see how the others are enjoying the Fourth of July," Sue told David. She moved close to him and put her arms around him. "Can I do that?"

"After I get a kiss," he replied.

Sue obliged and the two stood in the yard together, arms around each other, kissing. Unfortunately for them, their intimate moment was soon disrupted by the kids returning to the pool. Sue and David quietly smiled at each other and separated. David supervised the kids while Sue retrieved her laptop from her house.

Sue sat at the table on her porch. She enjoyed

the screened-in room with a view of the pool and David's backyard. The ceiling fan was especially nice in the heat of July. She opened her laptop, turned it on, and waited for her email messages to load.

She read the messages from Brandy, Martha and Janet. Each gave an update on their summer activities since they met three weeks ago.

Brandy started as a counselor in training at the Burbank YMCA. Denise was getting larger and more uncomfortable each week. Donald was enjoying making fun of Denise along with Juliana. But yet, he was, as Brandy wrote, "getting kinda weird and smoochy" with his wife.

Martha wrote that Patsy and Richard were spending a lot of time together. But Patsy was still her best barista buddy.

Janet and Larry were enjoying the hot weather, but did not at all like the "State Bird of Wisconsin," the mosquito.

And each asked for an update on the letters that Sue sent to the Secretary of the Interior.

Sue typed a response and addressed it to everyone:

Hello all!

I hope you have a special Independence Day holiday. It's so nice to celebrate another Independence Day. (Our first Independence Day was last November when Ted released us from the base!) The kids are so excited about the fireworks and I am too. We're going to have a fun night!

I know you are all wondering if I've heard anything from the Secretary of the Interior. I have not heard anything. No one has written me back. I hope that the Secretary actually got the letters. I suggest we write more letters. Send me some more ideas for things to say, and the children and I will write them up.

Happy 4th of July!

"There. Done," Sue announced to no one as she clicked the send button. She shut down her laptop, stood, and went out to visit the kids and David.

"What's for dinner, mommy?" Kati asked when Sue walked up to the edge of the pool.

"I don't know," Sue replied. "Probably soup, or maybe meatloaf."

"Yuck!" Kati and Violet both cried.

"Nuh uh, sister!" Karen called out. She had come over and jumped in the pool while Sue was checking email.

"When did we grow an extra child?" Sue asked David. "I thought we only had four."

"Mom says we're having burgers and hot dogs and cole slaw and potato salad and veggies and fruit and brownies," Karen told the other kids. "I helped make the brownies!" she proudly announced to Sue.

"There's no fooling you, is there little sister? You're right, we're having a good ol' American meal," Sue told the kids. "Speaking of which..." she turned to David, "shouldn't we get ready? Susan and Petunia will be here any minute."

"Yeah, okay. I guess we can start" As he and Sue reached his house, Susan and Petunia came around the corner carrying several dishes and bags of food. "You need some extra hands," David told them.

Susan replied, "We had a couple extra hands,

but she's currently swimming in the pool with your kids."

Sue and Susan carried the food into the kitchen while David went with Petunia across the street to her house to get the final load of food. When David and Petunia returned, the four adults took their time setting up. They were in no hurry. They wanted to enjoy the holiday.

After dinner and a baseball game in the yard (even the adults played), the sun began to set. Sue instructed the children to put on the long-sleeved shirts and jeans that she laid out, explaining how much mosquitoes love to bite little kids' arms and legs. Karen grabbed the bag of clothes her mother packed for her and went with the girls to their house to change. The adults changed too.

When everyone was dressed properly, they went around front to get in cars to go to the fireworks show. Petunia drove her car and Susan rode with her. David and Sue rode in the cab of his pick-up while the kids rode in the back.

"Are you sure this is a good idea?" Sue asked David as they started out the driveway. "Will the kids be safe riding in the back of the truck without belts?"

"They'll be fine. It's only six miles to Abilene and we'll be on route four fifty-two. We won't be going fast. It's not like we're on the interstate. There will be a lot of traffic and I'll drive slowly. I promise."

The two-car caravan started down the road to Abilene. The kids were excitedly singing songs and shouting.

Two hours later, around 11:00, the caravan safely returned to Enterprise. The kids could not stop talking about their first Fourth of July fireworks. Sue was excited too.

They all walked around David's garage to the back yard. David lit a small fire in his fire pit and everyone pulled up a chair.

The kids continued recalling the fireworks show, debating which kinds were the best and which ones were duds. Sue joined the discussion too. Her first fireworks celebration was just as memorable for her as it was for the kids.

David went to the garage freezer and brought out ice cream sandwiches for all. The conversation died down while everyone ate. And after eating, the silence remained as each quietly remembered the day.

Tyler was the first to fall asleep, followed by Kati and Karen. David carried Tyler into his house and Zachary stumbled after. Sue carried Kati and guided Violet into her house. Susan followed Sue, carrying Karen.

After tucking in all the children, Susan and Petunia said goodnight and walked around the garage to go home.

David and Sue stood in the middle of the back yard for a final goodnight. They gave each other one last hug and a long kiss before reluctantly going back to their respective houses.

Chapter 27 – The Right Thing

Sue woke, went downstairs and made herself coffee. She slept late for her--7:30. She knew the girls would sleep late after the long night before.

She moved out to her porch, hoping David would see her and join her. She turned on her computer and checked her email.

She was surprised to see she had responses to the email she sent the day before. Brandy, Patsy and Janet each responded to Sue.

Brandy replied in the afternoon and sent her idea for another letter. She wrote:

Mr. Secretary,

In my previous letter I suggested you use the internet to connect with teenagers on how to fix the environment. But in your messages, you and the government should ask teens to help out. We want to do our part for the environment. We want to help. We're ready to help. We'd feel included if we were asked to help. So please, Mr. Secretary, use the popular ways to communicate with teenagers to ask us to help with the government's efforts to clean the environment. And remember: You live on this planet, so clean up after yourself! Thank you Mr. Secretary.

Sincerely, Brandy Jackson

Patsy had replied to all after the fireworks, so the first half of her email was a review of the show and a description of the party Cupz hosted afterwards. She and Martha didn't get home until 2:30 in the morning, but she was so excited that she had to reply. The second half of her email was her next letter. Patsy wrote:

Dear Mr. Secretary,

All successful companies use very clever marketing campaigns to sell their products and ideas. Companies cannot be successful without them. Government agencies can also use advertising campaigns to successfully deliver messages; for example, Smokey the Bear's "Only you can prevent forest fires" and Nancy Reagan's "Just say no".

I remind you of the slogan we proposed previously in an effort to increase awareness for the environment: "You live on this planet. Clean up after yourself!" We believe that you could be quite successful using this slogan. We urge you to do so for the good of the environment.

Janet replied to Sue's email in the morning. She

wrote to Sue that she and Larry went to sleep just after the fireworks. They had a cook-out at their house and invited Mary. After eating, they watched the fireworks and called it a night. She and Larry enjoyed their first fireworks, but she admitted that they were feeling old and couldn't stay up too late. She wrote:

Mr. Secretary,

We'd like to remind you of the awareness campaign that we proposed a few weeks ago for addressing the environment: "You live on this planet, clean up after yourself!" It is very important that all of us in the U.S. help to clean up this planet. If we don't start, it will never get done.

We need your leadership, Mr. Secretary, to get the people of this country to clean up.

Thank you.

When she finished reading the email messages, Sue looked up to see David approach her porch. She was instantly filled with warmth. She stood and met him just outside the screen door where they hugged and kissed.

They eventually separated and Sue went inside to the kitchen to get David a cup of coffee. She returned and sat next to him on the glider on the porch. "When can we spend more nights with each other?" Sue whispered.

"You know we can't leave either the boys or the girls alone in one of the houses."

"I know," she sadly admitted. "But I want to spend more time with you."

"We talked about adding on to this house. We

could expand over this porch. I can use some of my savings to pay for the expansion. But we'd have to be certain it's the right thing to do for us and the kids. That's a big investment."

"It's the right thing to do," Sue told him, looking into his eyes. "I know it."

"You feel it's the right thing to do, and so do I." David responded, grasping and holding her hands. "But we have to look at this objectively. We need to make sure it's the correct decision. I don't know if we're ready to make that decision yet."

They didn't get the chance to discuss the idea further. The boys came running out of their house with a football. As they ran across the yard, they tossed the ball back and forth.

"Be careful of the pool, boys," David called.

"We are," Zachary replied.

"What's for breakfast?" Tyler shouted as he entered the porch.

"Please be quiet, boys," Sue responded in a loud whisper. "We don't want to wake the girls. If you'll come and sit here on the porch I'll get you some breakfast."

By the time she finished serving the boys and cleaned the dishes in the kitchen, the three girls came downstairs.

"Nine-thirty? You woke up pretty early for having gone to bed so late. Would you like some juice?" Sue asked the girls.

They each nodded and sat at the kitchen table. It was clear they weren't yet fully awake.

Sue served orange juice and sat down with them. "We need to write some more letters today," she began. "Can you help me?"

"Yeah, I guess so," Violet answered half-asleep.

"Not me," Karen replied. "I only know how to write English."

"I'll help as long as we can swim," Kati said. "The boys will help too, right? They can't play or swim without us."

"Yes, the boys will help," Sue responded, shaking her head at Kati, but also smiling at her competitiveness. "Can I make you something to eat?"

After the girls ate and Sue cleaned up the kitchen, she called the boys into the house. They sat at the kitchen table to write the letters. Sue showed the children the latest email messages and helped them write the letters on paper in their language. She also wrote a new letter herself. As usual, hers was more direct and to the point than the other letters. Sue didn't feel the need to waste a lot of words when the fate of the planet was in jeopardy.

When the letters were sealed in their envelopes and properly addressed to the Secretary of the Interior, Sue released the kids to go play outside.

Chapter 28 – They Got Lucky

The convertible sports car pulled into the parking lot of Manhattan Laboratory Services. A man in khaki pants and a Hawaiian shirt got out and walked to the entrance.

Jim Bailey opened the door and greeted his friend, "Hi Ted." He walked with Ted to the conference room where they joined Cindy, Sarah, and Bruno. Jim asked, "Can I get you anything?"

"Results," Ted replied with a smile.

"Coming right up." Jim pointed at Sarah to start the briefing.

"Hi Ted," Sarah said. "Welcome back. We've done a lot of testing since we saw you last. You're still looking good, by the way," she added with a wink. Ted thanked her. "We did all the logic tests that I think Jim told you about: the maze, the boxes, and the gerbil tubes. Amazing," she commented. "Anyways, we also conducted a lot of physiological tests on the cloned mice, their children and their grandchildren. We took the initial metabolism results as a cue of where to start.

We looked for other traits they have that might offer an advantage. We looked at all kinds of factors, especially environmental factors."

"We know from tests last year that they are all vulnerable to UV radiation," Cindy jumped in. "That's not new. But we also looked at exposure to heat. We put the mice under heat lamps in boxes for several minutes. We also put normal mice in identical boxes and monitored the temperature of the mice. We used infrared thermometers to measure the surface temperature of the mice. We found that the cloned mice and their descendents could cool themselves better than normal mice. Their skin stayed one to two degrees cooler. We repeated the experiment many times. We even put normal and cloned mice in the same box to eliminate sources of variability. In every experiment, the cloned mice remained cooler."

"We also looked at pollution and what effects it might have," Sarah continued. "We exposed the mice to smoke. We slowly increased the amount of smoke in the boxes and listened to the lungs of the mice every week." She laughed and added, "That was really tough to do. Anyway, each week, the normal mice's breathing became more raspy and congested. Their heart rate also seemed to increase too. But that's hard to measure accurately so it's hard to say if that was also a result. But the cloned mice and their descendents did not have anywhere near the same response. Only after all four weeks did we begin to detect any kind of congestion in their lungs. It appears that the transformed species has the ability to purify pollutants better than native species."

"There is more than just messaging in the clones," Bruno added.

"What does it all mean?" Ted asked. "What's the bottom line?"

"The clones could be the key to survival in a changing environment," Jim suggested.

Ted sat for a moment and then summarized, "So the extinct alien species from a planet that died a long time ago somewhere in the galaxy sent some goo to another planet in the hope that the goo would transform the planet's native species to have advantages on a planet that is getting hotter, more polluted and exposed to more radiation from its sun. Does that make sense?"

"Uh, I guess so," Jim replied.

Cindy said, "I wonder if the traits were intentionally engineered into the goo."

"Either way, intentional or not, the mice have these advantageous traits," Jim said.

"Advantageous?" Ted asked.

"Sure. The ability to control metabolism in times of plenty and famine and the ability to purify pollutants are both advantageous."

"What about exposure to UV radiation?" Ted challenged. "Getting your proteins scrambled doesn't seem like an advantage to me."

"It's more like a defense mechanism against cancer caused by too much radiation, like from the eroding hole in the ozone."

"But a lot of animals would have to die before the whole species would realize the vulnerability," Bruno observed.

"True," Jim replied.

"It's a good thing we discovered the protein scrambling as early as we did so our mice and the human clones didn't have to find out for themselves by getting skin cancer," Cindy told the others.

"Okay, so why did the alien species go extinct if they could engineer goo?" Sarah called out, diverting the conversation. "I mean, why not save your own species instead of saving some other species on another planet?"

Everyone sat and contemplated the question. *Why didn't they save themselves?*

After a few moments, Bruno offered a suggestion, "Perhaps there wasn't enough time to save themselves. Maybe they tried to incorporate new genes into their species, but there wasn't enough time for the genetic mutations to take hold across the whole species across the whole planet. That would have required too many generations."

"Why not clone new people?" Ted asked.

"Well…" Bruno began, "they… uh…"

"They could have," Sarah jumped in. "They could have cloned a few of their people, maybe hundreds or thousands. But they still wouldn't have had time for the mutations to take hold across the entire species before the planet became inhabitable."

"So they decided to clone another species on a planet that had more time to incorporate the mutations," Ted deduced. "Once incorporated, the mutations would offer the means of survival, means they couldn't have for themselves."

"Interesting," Jim responded.

"Very," Ted agreed.

"Hold on!" Cindy said. "How did they know to send the goo to Earth? How did they know how much time we had left?"

"They didn't. How could they know? It was just random," Sarah replied. "They just blasted a bunch of goo all over the galaxy and hoped that it landed someplace where it would work."

"So they got lucky," Cindy concluded.

"Maybe not," Jim replied. "A newer planet, galacticly-speaking, would have more time. They could have searched for regions in the galaxy with newer stars. Where there are newer stars, there are newer planets."

"But there are still millions of stars and millions of planets that would be newer than theirs," Bruno commented.

"Yeah," Cindy repeated, "they got lucky."

Chapter 29 – Can't You See?

When her shift ended at 2:30, Sue hung up her apron and bid farewell to everyone in the café. She smiled as she exited out the front door and walked around the side of the building to get her bike.

"Good afternoon, Ms. Cook. May we call you Suzanne?" a man in a black suit asked her.

"Who are you?"

"We're from the FBI," a second man in a black suit replied. "I'm Agent Manheim and he's Agent White."

"What do you want?" Sue asked nervously.

"Agent Manheim and I would like to have a few words with you, Suzanne," the first man told her. "May we escort you back to your house?"

"Do I have a choice?"

"Not really."

"Then yes, I guess you can."

Sue got on her bike and quickly rode to her house. She pulled into the driveway and into David's garage. When she skidded to a stop, she frantically called out for David.

David came out to the garage from his house. He immediately noticed the black sedan that was parked in his driveway. "What's going on?" he asked excitedly. "What did you do? What do they want?"

"I don't know!" Sue cried out. "They stopped me after work and asked to talk with me at my house." She nervously looked back to see the two men walking toward her, fear in her eyes. "I don't know what they want."

"Stay here," David quietly told her. "Do not go to your house. You can talk to them here in the garage."

"Good afternoon, sir," Agent White addressed David. "And you are?"

"David Hudson. I'm a friend."

"Would you please excuse us?" Agent White asked.

"If necessary," David replied. He stood with his arms folded and waited for a response.

"It is necessary," Agent White said.

David turned to go into his house. He told Sue, "I'll be just inside if you need me."

"Please stay close," Agent Manheim instructed David. "We'll want to talk to you too."

David nodded and went inside. He quickly went to his office on the other side of the house and called Ted. "Ted, this is David. We have an emergency. The FBI is here and they're interrogating Sue. Where are you? ... In Kansas? Really? Can you get here? ... Okay. Get here as fast as you can. ... Thanks Ted."

He hung up the phone and walked back to the garage. He opened the door and found Sue sitting in a folding lawn chair. The agents were standing over her.

"It wasn't until last week that we were able to translate your letters," Agent White said. "At least we now know the content."

"You were sending secret encrypted messages to a member of the federal government, Ms. Cook. Do you understand the magnitude of that crime? We can convict you of espionage against the United States," Agent Manheim threatened.

"Espionage?"

"Spying, Ms. Cook," Agent White replied.

"Spying?" Sue replied with surprise. "For writing letters suggesting ways to start an advertising campaign to save the planet?" she challenged.

"We don't care what you wrote, Ms. Cook. We care that you used a secret language. You cannot be trusted, Ms. Cook," Agent Manheim told her.

"And who are the other people you refer to in your letters?" Agent White asked. "You consistently used the word 'we.' Who are you working with? Give us their names."

"No. I will not," Sue defiantly replied. She folded her arms in front of her.

"No bother. We have the names of the others from the emails between you," Agent White smugly responded. "We hacked into your account and those of the others. We have enough information."

"We'll be able to convict all of you," Agent Manheim added with a grin.

"Are you serious?" Sue yelled, slamming her fists on the arms of the chair. "You're going to arrest me for writing letters? For writing letters suggesting that the people of this country clean up the planet? Everyone has got to do their part if we are going to fix the environment. We suggested a new campaign. You live on this planet! Clean up after yourself! That's all we're doing. We're not spies! We're not a threat! We want everyone to save the planet! Can't you see? If people don't do their part, no one will do what it takes! The planet will slowly die and all of us on it will too!"

"We don't care why you wrote your letters," Agent Manheim said. "You wrote the letters to a government official, to a member of the President's cabinet, in a secret code that had to be broken by the FBI. These letters and your emails are enough for us to send you all to prison for espionage and conspiracy."

"You can't be serious," David argued, jumping into the conversation.

"We are, Mr. Hudson. And we expect you to stay out of this issue," Agent Manheim replied.

"Now if you'll excuse us, we have a report to file," Agent White said. "We'll be in touch with you soon. Do not leave the country, Ms. Cook."

"Where do you think I would go?"

"Just stay here. We'll contact you shortly," Agent White told her.

The two agents turned and walked to their car. Sue and David watched as they pulled out of the driveway and drove off.

Sue hugged David, buried her head in his chest, and began to cry. David realized this was the first time he had ever seen Sue cry. He pulled her even closer and hugged a little tighter.

"That was horrible," Sue sobbed. "How can they think we're spies? We did nothing wrong. We just wrote letters. So what if we used our language. We gave them the code. We just wanted to get the Secretary's attention."

"Oh you got his attention alright," David quietly replied. "And the rest of the government too."

Sue looked into David's eyes. "Do you think they'll arrest us?"

"I don't think so. But I don't know. The FBI has to know who you clones are. So maybe things are different for you. I don't know."

"I have to tell the others," she said with determination, wiping the tears from her eyes. "I have to email them right away."

"They'll intercept your emails."

"I don't care. I have to tell the others what happened. They've got to know."

They stood in the garage holding each other. Sue was still shaking when Ted's convertible pulled into the driveway. He got out and briskly walked to Sue and David.

"You're too late, I'm afraid. They left already," David told him.

"I'm sorry I couldn't get here sooner," Ted responded sincerely. "Let's go sit out back and you can tell me about it."

As they walked to the back patio, Ted asked, "Where are the kids?"

"They're over with Karen at Susan's house. Petunia is watching them. They're doing some arts and crafts," David answered.

"Thank goodness they didn't hear or see any of that," Sue added, still wiping the tears from her eyes.

"So what exactly did they say to you?" Ted asked as they took seats.

"They said they could put me in prison for being a spy," Sue replied. "I don't like them." She became disgusted with the agents as she recalled the conversation.

"They told Sue they could convict her of espionage for writing coded messages to a member of the Cabinet," David clarified. "And they knew about Brandy and Patsy and the others from hacking into email accounts. They said the others could also be convicted of conspiracy."

"They're right, you know," Ted replied. "Technically they can convict you all. But in a case of domestic espionage, as opposed to foreign espionage, convictions are more difficult. And in a case like this, where the letters obviously aren't threatening anyone or making demands, it would be nearly impossible to convict you."

"Then why did they come here and threaten me?" Sue asked.

"I don't exactly know," Ted replied. "They probably just want you to stop sending coded messages to the Secretary. They just wanted to scare you."

"Can't they just ask instead of threatening to put me in prison?"

"Would you just say 'Okay' and stop writing?" Ted asked.

"No," Sue admitted, shaking her head. "I probably wouldn't."

"So they have to come here in person and scare the begeebers out of you to get you to stop," Ted told her. "You probably aren't in any real trouble, but I suggest you stop writing letters."

"Why? We should not stop until the Secretary of the Interior gets the message and starts the campaign. It's too important!"

"He may never get the message and never start the campaign," Ted informed her. "That's not how things work in the government."

"Why not?"

"It just doesn't, Sue. I can't explain it to you. It's just too complicated."

"That's stupid!" she protested. She rose up out of her chair and stomped her foot with her fists at her side. She insisted, "The Earth is way too important for government officials to ignore. I don't care how much money it costs or who has to pay. The planet has to be saved! It's obvious! Everyone can see that we all need to do our part. Why can't the government see that?"

"They can see it," Ted calmly said. He looked up at Sue standing over him and added, "They just don't want to admit it. And they don't want to be reminded about it either."

Chapter 30 – Other Ways

Brandy opened her email account and looked through her inbox. She noticed a message from Sue with the subject of "Warning–FBI is watching."

"Uh oh," she said out lout.

"What's wrong, kid?" Donald asked.

"I got an email from Sue. We all did. She sent it to all of us."

"Why is that bad?" he asked. "What does it say?"

"The subject is 'Warning, the FBI is watching.'"

"Oh." Donald put his book down. "C'mon." He motioned for Brandy to follow him to the balcony.

Donald opened the screen door and allowed Brandy to exit first. They sat down next to Denise. "We have something you should probably see," he told Denise. "And you better call Juliana, too."

"What is it?" Denise asked.

"An email from Sue," Brandy replied. "The subject is 'Warning, the FBI is watching.'"

"Call Juliana," Denise told Donald.

Donald went into the kitchen and called Juliana. He invited her to dinner, if she didn't already have plans, and told her about the email from Sue. When he hung up he announced, "She's on her way over right now."

"What does Sue's email say?" Denise asked.

"I'll read it to you," Brandy said. "Hi all. I want you to know that the FBI came to see me today."

Donald looked at Denise with shock and concern. Brandy noticed his expression. "Is that bad?" she asked.

"I don't know," Denise calmly replied. "Keep reading and we'll see."

Brandy continued, "Two agents threatened me. They know about our letters. They know about us. They didn't care about what we wrote. But they did care that we wrote to a government official and used our special language. They say they can arrest and convict us of espionage and conspiracy."

"Oh my," Denise said. "She must have been scared to death. That's awful." She reached out and held Donald's hand.

Brandy read on, "Ted was here but he arrived after the FBI left. He wasn't very supportive of us. He was more on the side of the government, or maybe not. I can't tell for sure. He didn't think the FBI would actually arrest us, but he suggested we stop writing letters."

"So Ted was there and told us to stop writing letters?" Donald confirmed.

"Yeah, but there's more in Sue's email," Brandy told him. She continued reading, "I suggest we continue to write letters. We're not even sure the Secretary of the Interior read the message. How do we know anything will be done? We can't just quit. The environment is too important to quit. I'm not going to let the FBI come here and scare me. I don't want to be arrested, but I don't think they will arrest me. I want to keep writing until we see the government take action and start a campaign. Are you with me? Will you help write more letters?"

After Brandy finished reading Sue's letter, she and Donald and Denise sat on the balcony in silence, thinking about the situation. *Sue almost got in trouble because of the letters. The FBI certainly scared her. And now she wants to keep writing letters? Even after Ted suggested they didn't???* They didn't know how to react to her email message. *We can't keep writing letters and get arrested, but we can't abandon Sue and we can't abandon the campaign to clean up the planet. The environment is too important.*

As they sat in silence, Juliana burst into the apartment. "Did you read Sue's email?" she asked excitedly. "What are we going to do?"

"We're just thinking about that right now," Donald replied.

"I say we keep writing letters," Brandy announced. "I agree with Sue. The environment is too important."

"But sweetie, you could be arrested," Denise replied. "We could all be arrested."

"We *do not* want to be arrested," Juliana firmly stated. "We'd lose our jobs, especially if it was for espionage and conspiracy."

"If I lost my job, I couldn't work anywhere else," Donald said, looking to Denise. "Who would hire a man with no employment or education history who got fired from a government job because he was arrested?"

"There's no way I'll let myself get arrested. I have a new baby on the way!" Denise exclaimed.

Brandy stammered, "But the environment--"

"Is not more important than our family," Denise told her. "You must realize this. Sue must realize this."

The phone rang.

"I'll get it," Juliana offered. She walked into the kitchen and picked up the receiver. "Hello? ... Patsy! It's me, Juliana. I'm here with the others." She walked out onto the patio. "Yes, we just read Sue's email. ... It is terrible, I agree. We're just talking about that right now. ... We don't know what we're going to do. We could lose our government jobs and we can't afford that. ... I know we have to support Sue, but it sounds like she's going to write more letters."

"We should write back and tell Sue not to write any more letters," Denise loudly responded so Patsy could hear her voice over the phone. "She'll put herself and all of us in jeopardy."

After listening to Patsy, Juliana told the others, "Patsy agrees. We should write to Sue and tell her to not write any more letters."

"Okay. Tell Patsy to write to Sue," Denise instructed Juliana. "We will too. I hope Sue gets the message."

Juliana walked back into the kitchen while she talked. "Patsy? ... Write back to Sue, okay? We'll do it too. ... Okay, that sounds good. Nice talking to you Patsy. ... We'll talk soon. ... Okay, bye."

While Juliana hung up the phone, Brandy checked her email for more messages. "Janet replied too," she told the others.

"What'd she say, sis?" Juliana asked.

Scanning the message, Brandy replied, "She's scared... Mary says that it's not good the FBI visited Sue... She doesn't think we should write more letters... She wants to know what we should do."

"Reply to her and tell her what we talked about with Patsy. Tell her she should reply to Sue," Denise told her.

"Okay." Brandy started typing. In a few minutes she finished writing the reply to Janet and clicked the send button. "There. Done. Should we write to Sue now?"

"How about if we help you write and proofread it before you send it to Sue?" her mother suggested. "This message is pretty important."

"Duh! I know what to write, Mom. Sheez!"

"I know, sweetie, but this is really important." Denise said.

Juliana added, "We have to send the right message of support to Sue, but we have to convince her not to send any more messages. We have to be nice, but also firm, in the same message. Does that make sense?"

"Yeah, I get it. I can handle it." Brandy started typing the reply to Sue. She kept putting her hand up in the air to keep her mother from making comments while she typed. She was quite confident she could write the reply.

When she finished, she read the message out loud to the others. "Yo, Sue. We are so sorry that you had to deal with the FBI. I'm glad David was there for you. And it's good that Ted showed up and helped you. We want to help you, but we also want all of us to be safe. None of us want to go to jail. So we don't want you to write more letters to the Secretary of the

Interior. Yes, we all think the environment is very important. I especially think so. And so do my friends. But I don't want to go to jail and neither do Jules or Don or Mom. And Mom has a baby! The baby would go to jail too. They would all lose their jobs. It would really be bad. We really do want to write letters about the environment. But there are other ways to get the message out. Please don't send other messages, Sue. We'll spread the word about the environment in other ways, I promise. Your friends always, Brandy, Donald, Denise and Juliana."

"That was very well written," Denise praised.

"That rocked, dude! Nice!" Juliana added, giving Brandy a high-five.

"Thanks," Brandy replied.

"Click the button and send it to Sue," Donald said.

Chapter 31 – Not Just You

"I don't know what to do," Sue said to David. "They all say that I should not send more letters. It's too dangerous."

"It is," David agreed. "You could get yourself and everyone else convicted of a crime and sent to prison. Do you want that? Do you want that for the children? Do you want that for Brandy? Do you want that for Denise's baby?"

"No. But the environment is important."

"It's not *that* important," David insisted. "It's not important enough to endanger your family and friends."

"I know… but--"

"But nothing, Sue! You cannot risk the lives of your family and friends! It's not just you. It's twenty other people too!"

"I know. Okay."

But David wasn't convinced she was okay.

Chapter 32 – Take Care of This

Ted arrived ten minutes late for the committee meeting. When he entered the room, General Gilmore announced, "Finally!"

Ted walked to his chair.

"Are you avoiding us, Ted? Is that why you're late?" the general barked.

"The driver you sent to pick me up got stuck in traffic. He must be a rookie. He didn't know where to go. It's not my fault."

"Sit down."

Ted did as he was told. He shifted in the chair to get comfortable.

In his abrasive voice, the general asked, "Can you please explain to this committee what the hell is going on? We have two sets of letters written by your damn aliens! The FBI had to visit the one in Kansas to scare the crap out of her. Your aliens are threatening the Secretary and practically taunting the FBI to lock them up!"

"They are not threatening the Secretary."

"Oh really! And you know this how, may I ask?" Mr. Wright snapped.

"I know them. They would not threaten the Secretary. And they are not taunting the FBI. They are simply writing letters."

"In their coded language! This is espionage!" Mr. Wright bellowed.

"Espionage, huh? Did you happen to translate the letters?" Ted asked.

"Yes, we did," Mr. Mason replied.

"Can I see them?"

The general held out the papers. Ted stood up and walked over to him to take them. He read the translated messages as he slowly walked back to his chair. He sat and finished reading. "There are no threats in here," he told the committee. "There's no way you can actually think that requests for a publicity campaign can be considered espionage."

"Unsolicited communication with government officials in coded language is a matter of security. We have to assume this is a threat," The general replied.

"Have *you* read these?" Ted asked the general. "Obviously you haven't," he said shaking his head. "There's nothing in them. There are no threats. There's no malicious intent. They simply wanted to get the Secretary's attention."

"They did," Mr. Wright said, "as well as the FBI's attention too."

"Get control of these people, Ted!" the general ordered. "Get control of these aliens or we will." He paused and added, "You never know what the FBI is planning. I can't speak for the FBI, you know. They may already be planning something. Do something now, or somebody else will, Ted. I promise you that."

"I'll start with the Secretary. I'll talk to him. Do you mind if I do that?" Ted asked politely.

They shook their heads and each replied, "No."

Ted stood up and placed the copies of the letters in his portfolio. "I'll take care of this."

Chapter 33 – Another Letter

Sue woke up early on Saturday. The girls were still asleep. She took her coffee cup and computer to the front porch. She looked across the yard toward David's house for several moments, but couldn't see any movement. She wished she could have some quiet time with him, but it wasn't to be.

She sat on the glider, opened her computer and read her email messages. In the two weeks since the FBI visited her, communications between the clones settled back to near normal. Emails messages stopped containing anything about the letters and the 'Clean Up After Yourself!' campaign.

Sue couldn't help being annoyed. She knew that the others didn't want her to write any more letters. And she knew they were right. But something inside her wouldn't let go. Just like last year when she stowed away in the back of the delivery van, she knew she had a message to deliver. And she was determined to deliver it, no matter what the consequences.

I can't put my friends in danger. I can't put my children

in danger! But I can't let the earth stay in danger. I have to do something. I have to get the message out.

She suddenly had an idea. "I'll ask Ted if we can all get together," she said out loud. "Then we can act as a large group; power in numbers."

Sue typed a quick message to Ted asking if they could all travel back to Kansas before school started. She argued that the clones could use the visit to find a way to get the message out with making the FBI angry. And it would just be fun to see each other again.

"There. That should do it," she said when she clicked the send button.

But will that be enough? What if we can't meet for two more weeks? That might be too much time. The Secretary may forget about us. He may forget the slogan. If we take too much time, the idea will fade.

Sue went inside and got paper and a pencil. She sat down and composed another letter. She did not bother writing the letter in the clones' language. She knew there was no longer any reason to write in code. She wanted the Secretary to read it first before the FBI took it away. *The Secretary needs to get this message:*

Dear Mr. Secretary,

I am sending one final letter to ask you to consider our advertising campaign.

I don't know if you know who we are. I will tell you. We are eleven people who were cloned from an alien substance that was sent to Earth last year. Mr. Ted Stevens was assigned to bring us together on the base in California. We lived there for a while. During that time, I received a message. I don't know how I got it, but it told me I had to deliver it. I escaped from the base and went back to Kansas. I told them that I am the memory of an extinct species from a dead planet in the galaxy. The alien species could not save themselves, so they sent the substance to help other people on other planets survive. The eleven of us are the messengers for that species. We are also messengers for the planet.

Everyone needs to work to save the planet. It is not just a good idea, it's necessary. The other clones and I, along with family and friends, want to get the message out to everyone that we are all responsible for saving the planet and saving ourselves. We suggest the slogan "You live on this planet. Clean up after yourself!" We need your help to spread the message. We want to live on a healthy planet.

Thank you,
Suzanne Cook.

She folded the letter and placed it in an envelope. She addressed it to the Secretary and included her return address. She put the envelope under a stack of junk mail on her kitchen counter, hiding it until she could mail before work on Monday.

Chapter 34 – Is She Joking?

What the hell is she thinking? Get together? When everyone in Homeland Security is paying attention?

Ted sat at his desk, wearing a black suit and black tie.

"She's out of her mind," he replied out loud. "She's absolutely crazy."

He was completely baffled. *Can she be serious? Is she joking?*

He shook his head and rubbed his face with his hands. He couldn't deal with her request. He left her email unanswered.

Chapter 35 – Crazy Things

After dinner on Friday night, while cleaning Sue's kitchen, David asked her, "I thought we could pitch the tents in the backyard and let the kids sleep out there tonight. That would give us some time to spend alone, together, at night. What do you think?"

"I… uh… yeah, okay," Sue replied. Her thoughts were somewhere else.

"What's wrong with you? You've been distant all week. Are you sick? What's going on?"

Sue snapped to attention and came back to the present. "I'm sorry. I've been thinking about all that's happened. What was it you said?"

"I offered to pitch a tent in the yard for the kids. But that's not important right now. What is it that has you thinking so hard?"

"Oh, it's nothing. I just sent an email to Ted and he never responded. He always responds to my email messages. But he didn't respond to the last one."

"What did you write?" David asked. "You aren't still going on about the letters are you?"

"No. I just asked if all of us clones could get together again this summer before school starts."

David broke into laughter. "Well no wonder!"

"What?"

"After all this stuff about the letters and the FBI and all that, Ted's probably feeling a lot of pressure to do something to fix the situation."

"From who?" Sue inquired.

"From the Department of Homeland Security, the FBI, and maybe even the Secretary of the Interior. The last thing he needs is for all of you to be in one place together."

"Why?"

"What happens when you all get together?" David asked, pushing her to think about the right answer.

"We have fun. We talk. We drink a lot of coffee. We--"

"You get messages," David reminded her. "The last thing Ted needs is for you all to get some new message and start doing new crazy things to get him in trouble."

"Crazy things? We don't do crazy things! We do things to spread our messages," Sue replied defensively. She folded her arms and glared at him.

"I didn't mean it that way, Sue," David said, placing a hand on her shoulder. "I'm sorry. I meant crazy as in unique, or different."

"You're picking on us and making fun of us and I don't appreciate it. There's a reason why we're here and we're not going to stop doing our 'crazy things!'"

David pulled Sue close and put his arms around her. She did not resist, but did not relax.

"I don't know what's going on in your brilliant

mind," he said, "but I'd like to help you. I know you're special. I know you have messages. But you're also a mother, and a… girlfriend. Come back to Kansas from wherever you are. Come back here to your house and your daughters. Come back here to me."

Sue looked up into David's eyes. The tension in her body ebbed. "I'm sorry," she said. "I guess I got a little too worked up. But it's not like Ted to ignore me. And that makes me nervous."

"There's nothing to worry about," David reassured her. "He's busy. He's got a lot to do. And last time he was here, he wasn't concerned. He just told you not to write any more letters. So it's alright. There's no reason to be concerned. You haven't written any other letters, so there's no reason for him to be mad or avoid you or anything like that. He's just busy."

Sue heard what David said, but all she could think about was the last additional letter she wrote. *Does he know that I wrote it? Does the FBI know? Am I in trouble? Are the others going to be in trouble? I think I messed up. Why did I write that letter?*

"C'mon. Let's go sit down," David suggested.

"I think I need to send an email to the others. Maybe that will help me feel better," Sue responded.

"Go ahead," he replied. Before she went upstairs to get her computer, David asked, "Can I pitch the tents for the kids tonight?"

Sue stopped and looked back at him with a small smile. "Please. That would be nice."

David left Sue's house and walked through the yard to get the tents from his garage. He had to call time-out to break up the game. He didn't actually know what the game was. The kids had a football, Frisbees and a plastic baseball bat. From what he could tell, the object of the game was to golf the football with the bat and run to the next Frisbee base before the opponent could touch the football. But he didn't bother to ask. He simply called a time-out and asked if they all wanted to sleep in the yard tonight. They all agreed, including Karen.

Sue brought her laptop out and sat the glider on her porch. She clicked to her email account and wrote a message to her fellow clones:

Hello all,

I wanted to tell you all something. You don't need to do anything. I just wanted to tell you. I sent an email to Ted asking if we could get together before school started. He didn't reply. He always replies to my email messages. I don't know if he is busy or if he's mad at me. I can't tell.

That's all I had to say. You know Ted as well as I do. Do you think it means anything? I hope it's nothing.

Your friend always, Sue

David called the kids. "Change your clothes to whatever you're going to sleep in. I have flashlights for you and some snacks. You can stay up as late as you want, but you have to be quiet. I don't want calls from the neighbors. Okay?"

They all agreed to the terms and scattered to change their clothes.

When they returned, David met them at the tents that were between his patio and the pool. After last-minute reminders, he zipped up the tents.

He walked to Sue's house. She was not on the porch, nor in the kitchen, nor in the living room. He turned out the lights downstairs and went up to her bedroom. Sue was in bed waiting for him.

He crawled in behind Sue and snuggled up close. He held her close and tight.

"I have something to tell you," Sue said.

"Yes?" David replied, anticipating a romantic suggestion.

"I wrote another letter."

David's arms relaxed around Sue. He sighed. "What are we going to do with you, Sue?"

Chapter 36 - Furious

Ted's cell phone rang at 8:00 in the morning. He had been awake for nearly two hours. He had tried to go back to sleep, but instead, he laid awake in bed staring at the ceiling. He had a lot on his mind. He picked up the phone and answered it.

"Hello?"

"Ted!" It was the general. He was yelling so loud that Ted had to hold the phone away from his ear.

"Your goddamn aliens sent another letter! The Secretary showed it to the FBI last night! It wasn't even encrypted! They just sent the damn thing as is! The FBI is furious, Ted! They're going to go get the one in Kansas and maybe all the others! You really screwed up on this one Ted! This is not going to look good when the dust settles! I suggest you get your ass in gear and do what you can to help! Now!"

The call ended.

Ted sighed deeply. His head now pounded. Virtual ice picks repeatedly jabbed into the side of his head.

"What did she do now?"

He lay in bed with his arms and legs splayed out. He stared at the ceiling once again. *She wrote another letter? After everyone told her not to? She didn't even use her language. And the Secretary gave it to the FBI. He had to. He couldn't sit on it. The bureau has got to be fuming about this. Sue... Sue... Sue...*

Finally he crawled out of bed, and stumbled to the bathroom. He took four Motrin and climbed in the shower. He stood in the hot water, dazed.

Chapter 37 – Two Weeks

Sue skidded to a stop in the garage. She greeted David with "Hi" as she hurried to her house. David had to run to keep up with her.

"I know how to fix it. I know how to make Ted happy. I'll write another email and apologize. I'll promise never to write another letter. And I'll tell him I mean it. He'll believe me if I really promise. I know he will. He's got to."

"I hope you're right," David replied skeptically.

"Ted trusts me. He likes me. He won't be mad at me."

David waited on the porch while Sue ran in and retrieved her computer. She didn't even bother to change her clothes. She came back out on the porch and sat with David on the glider. She powered up and launched her email program. At the top of her inbox she saw a message from Ted.

Shocked, she said, "He sent a message!"

"Read it," David responded.

"It's addressed to everyone," Sue noted. She

read the message aloud, "In two weeks I will pick you up in my plane. Arrangements are being made. I cannot go into details."

David and Sue looked at each other with confusion and concern. David moved closer to Sue.

She continued to read, "I will pick up Janet, Larry, and Mary in Wisconsin, then everyone in Kansas, including David, Karen, Susan, and Petunia. Then we'll fly to Arizona to pick up Patsy, Richard, and Martha. We'll fly to California to meet up with the others. You all know about the letter-writing campaign, that's why Mary, David, Susan, Karen, Petunia, Richard, Juliana, and Denise must accompany the clones. You do not need any supplies. In a few days I will give you exact times for when you will be picked up. Do not tell anyone about this email. Do not mention this to anyone. And do not send any more letters! I cannot give you any more details, so please do not email me or call me. I will not respond."

Sue turned to face David. "What does this mean?" she asked.

"I don't know," David replied quietly. "I have no idea."

"Is it bad? Are we going back to the base? Are they locking us all up? Are we going to jail?" With each question she asked, Sue became more agitated. "They can't lock us up! And they can't lock up Karen and Susan and Petunia! They can't lock up Richard or Mary. They can't lock you up! Oh, what have I done? It's all my fault!"

David placed his hands on her shoulders to settle her. "Calm down, Sue. It'll be okay. Do not panic. I'm sure there is an explanation."

"They're taking us all back to the base in

California! All of us who know about the letters!"

"Sue, please. There might be an explanation for this besides what you think."

"What is it?" she snapped.

"I don't know," David calmly replied. "Let's not panic. Let's try to think about this."

The kids heard Sue's response to Ted's email. They got out of the pool and came in the porch wrapped in towels.

Sue's phone rang. She ran into the kitchen to answer it. The others listened from the porch.

"Hello? … Yes, I just read it. … I don't know, Patsy. I don't know what it means. … Maybe they're taking us all back to the base. … Yes, even Richard. You read the email. He included them because they all know about the letters! … I think they can do whatever they want. … Call Denise tonight after they get off work. Then call me or email me back. I want to know what she thinks. And Juliana too. … Okay Patsy. Talk to you soon. … Goodbye."

The children became very nervous. "Are we going back?" Violet asked.

"I don't know," Sue replied. "Mr. Stevens said we're going to California. He's picking us all up in the plane like he did before."

"I'm not going back," Violet insisted.

"Neither am I," Zachary added. "No way."

"Me neither," Tyler added. "They can't take me away from here! I won't go!"

"Calm down boys," David said quietly. "All of you, please stay calm. There is an explanation. I don't know what it is yet, but they are not going to lock all of us up at the base."

"Then what are they going to do?" Kati asked.

Taking her cue from David, Sue took a couple deep breaths to calm herself in front of the children, and then quietly responded, "Mr. Stevens is picking all of us up in his plane and we're flying to California. That's all we know right now, sweetie. We'll know more later," she reassured Kati.

"I'm sure it's not bad," David added with confidence. "Go swimming again until dinner. There's nothing to worry about."

The kids, reluctantly believing their parents, agreed they were done swimming. They each slowly went to their own bedroom to change clothes.

Sue and David stayed sitting on the glider on the porch. "I should email everyone," Sue announced.

"Don't," David sternly replied. He held her hands and looked in her eyes. "Let's not get everyone excited or make this worse by sending a whole bunch of emails back and forth. Let's wait until Patsy calls back tonight and see what she and Denise and Juliana talked about."

"But--"

"But nothing, Sue. Don't make things worse. If you want, you can go call Janet and Larry in an hour when they get home. But no emails. Not yet."

Sue nodded and leaned against David. "I don't want to go back. I can't go back," she said with tears in her eyes.

David put his arm around her and held her tight. He wanted to be a pillar of strength and confidence for Sue. But thinking about the possibilities and what they could mean while Sue was crying into his shirt almost made *him* break down. *What is Ted doing? There has to be an explanation. Another reunion? No. There'd be no reason for secrecy. A surprise? Maybe, but what?*

What could it be? Is it really relocation? Are we all being relocated to the base? He couldn't find an explanation other than relocation, and it scared him. He sat quietly, holding Sue tightly, trying to shake the idea of relocating out of his head.

After several minutes of silence, David finally said, "Come on." He sat up and gently pushed Sue up. He brightened his face to try to change the mood. "Let's go swimming. We can float together and…" he added, breaking into a grin, "hold each other."

"I don't know."

"It'll be relaxing for you, for both of us. Let's go get our suits on."

"Okay. I guess."

"Can I help you get changed?" he asked, feigning innocence. He playfully tried to break her attention.

Sue realized what he intended and snapped, "No! Not with the kids around! You go to your house and change."

"Dang it."

Chapter 38 – Going Back

After the swim, Sue was much more relaxed. She made a big dinner and they all ate well. Just as they finished, the phone rang.

"Hi Janet. I'm so glad you called. ... Yes, I read Ted's email. ... I don't know what it means. David and I have thoughts about it, but we don't know. What does Mary think? ... If she doesn't know what it means, then Ted is being very careful. She's really smart and knows Ted, so if Mary doesn't know what's going on, then none of us do. ... The only thing we can do is wait for two more weeks. ... I don't like that either, but there's nothing else we can do. ... We'll stay in touch by email and phone. ... That sounds good. Give our best to Larry and Mary. We'll talk to you soon. ... Goodbye Janet."

"Let me guess, that was Janet?" David asked.

"Obviously," Sue replied.

"What did she say?" Violet inquired.

"Not much. She was just trying to find out what Ted's message meant. Not even Mary knows what's going on." She turned to David, "Should Mary know what's going on?"

"Probably not, since she was in on the letters," he replied. "Something is happening for those of us who know about the letters."

Sue sat in her chair at the dining table with the others. No one said anything. They didn't know what to say. They just thought about the situation.

The silence was broken by another phone call. Sue answered and put the phone on speaker so everyone could hear the conversation.

"Denise! How are you?"

"Fine. We're fine," Denise replied.

"How's the baby?" Sue asked.

"The baby is good. It's starting to kick pretty hard."

"We're all so excited for you. Of course, we're not as excited as you and Donald must be. How's Brandy enjoying her summer? Did she like being a counselor in training?"

"Yes, she did. Now it's time to get ready for school," Denise replied. Abruptly, she asked, "Did you get Ted's email?"

"Yes, I got it," Sue flatly replied. Her mood changed at the mention of Ted.

"What do you think?"

"We can't figure it out," Sue responded, looking at David and the kids sitting in the dining room with her. "And I just talked to Janet, and she and Mary don't know either. The only thing I can think of is he's going to take us back to the base. What does Juliana think?"

"We don't think it means we're going back to the base," Denise said.

"David doesn't think so either," Sue told her. "But then, what can it be? They wouldn't take you and Juliana and Richard and David and Susan and Petunia. And Karen! They wouldn't take all of you to the base."

"I agree. Ted and the FBI can't come in and take us from our homes. They can't take us from our jobs and our schools. What would our friends say? What would our neighbors say? What would the kids' teachers say?"

"Mr. Stevens might take us clones," Sue acknowledged, "but not you, especially not with a new baby!"

"I don't think he will take anyone back to the base," Denise responded. But there was skepticism in her voice.

"It doesn't make sense. But then, what could it be? What could the email mean?" Sue repeated.

"I don't know," Denise admitted.

"We should all stay in touch," Sue suggested.

"Yes, I agree. And please don't send Ted an email, Sue."

"No, I won't. I promise," Sue replied. "His email was pretty clear that he wasn't going to respond. So I won't bother sending him an email. But I don't like not knowing."

"Neither do I, but until Ted tells us, we won't know."

Denise's response did not make Sue feel any better. "If you get any ideas, please call us, okay?" Sue pleaded.

"I will," Denise said.

"Okay. Take care of you and your little baby. Goodbye Denise."

"Goodbye Sue."

Sue hung up the phone. She sighed and stared down at the floor, thinking about the situation.

"So what's going to happen?" Kati asked.

"I don't know! No one docs!" Sue barked.

Kati began to cry, and immediately Sue realized what she had done. She went to her knees in front of Kati's chair. Tears welled up in her eyes as she looked at Kati crying. Speaking softly, she said, "I'm sorry dear. I didn't mean to yell at you. I am so sorry. I'm frustrated and scared." She told Kati and the others. "I don't know what Mr. Stevens has planned. It might be just a visit. But it might mean we're all going back to the base. And that scares me. It really scares me."

"Don't be scared, Mommy," Violet replied. "It will be alright. That's what you always tell us."

"This time I'm not sure," Sue told her daughters. "This time I don't know. I don't want you all to have to grow up on that base. Not after all that we've done. And what about the others, like Richard and Susan and Karen? They were just helping us." She sat on the floor and openly started to cry.

The children crowded around to console her. David joined her sitting on the floor and the kids followed his lead, sitting next to Sue.

"Independence," Sue sobbed. "That's all we want. We don't want to harm anyone or cause any trouble. We just want to live free on a planet that won't die? Why can't they see that? Why can't they see that all we want to do is tell people to clean up the planet? We're just trying to do what's right and now it's all for nothing. We're going back to the base. And innocent people are going to be forced to go back with us."

Chapter 39 – Sounds Familiar

A week after receiving Ted's email and a week before travel day, suspense had been building at Sue's house. The previous week had been spent calling California, Arizona and Wisconsin, and everyone was unsure about what was to happen the next week. With each day, the suspense and uncertainty grew.

Kati and Violet woke in the morning around 9:00, their usual time in the summer. They went downstairs and each made a bowl of cereal. They turned on the TV and watched cartoons. In a few minutes or so, they knew David would come over and check in on them. He always did when their mom had to work.

As expected, David entered the house around 9:15. However, he did not greet the girls with his usual smile and cheerful "Hello." He slowly walked up to the kitchen counter carrying an envelope, silently reading the note that was inside. He hardly acknowledged the girls. He took a seat on a stool and whispered, "How can she be so naïve? How can she think that'll work?"

"What's wrong, David?" Violet asked.

"Uh... nothing," he said, as he folded the letter and put it back in the envelope. "Nothing," he repeated. Changing his expression to a happy face, he asked the girls, "How did you two sleep last night?"

"Good," Kati replied.

"What's in the letter?" Violet asked. She watched David read it. She knew it bothered him. "Is it from Mom?"

"Yes," he admitted. "Your mom wrote the letter."

"What does it say?" Violet continued.

David paused before responding. He sighed. "It says that she left to go to Washington D.C. She wants to talk to the Secretary of the Interior to put things right. She wants to apologize so we all don't have to be taken away by Ted."

"Mommy left?" Kati asked with tears forming in her eyes. "She just left us? She went away? Why?"

"It's okay, Kati," David reassured her. "She went to go talk to the man that she sent the letters to. She wants to talk to him in person. But I don't think she's traveled very far this morning. We'll find her and ask her to come home."

"I'm worried," Kati cried.

"Don't be," David said quietly. He walked up to her and knelt down to be at her eye level. "Your mother is fine. Nothing will happen, I promise. She'll be back soon."

"Okay," Kati responded. But she wasn't convinced.

"I'll call Deputy Leland. You remember Spike, right? He'll find your mother."

David pulled his cell phone out of his pocket

and dialed. "Spike? ... It's David Hudson. ... Fine. Listen, Sue has left her house to go to Washington D.C. ... She has another message to deliver. ... Yeah, she left a note. ... She can't have gotten very far. I bet if you put out an APB, you'll find her in Topeka, or Lawrence, or Kansas City. ... Thanks Spike. Call me when you know anything."

"What's an APB?" Kati asked.

"It's an all-points bulletin. It means that police should keep an eye out for your mother. If anyone finds her, they'll call Spike."

"Are they going to arrest her?" Violet asked.

"No. They'll find her and bring her home," he said confidently. "Why don't you two come over to my house and you and the boys can watch TV together?"

The girls agreed. They wanted to be close to David and definitely not alone. They turned off the TV, put their cereal bowls in the sink and walked with David to his house.

The kids gathered around the TV in the living room and started watching cartoons. Zachary and Tyler sat on the couch and put their feet up on the coffee table, unaware of the situation. Kati and Violet could not relax. Their missing mother troubled them.

David nervously sat in the kitchen. After a while, he couldn't sit any longer. He started pacing back and forth, waiting for Spike to call. Finally, his phone rang.

"What's going on Spike? ... They found her? Oh, thank god. Where is she? ... How'd she get to Topeka? ... Delivery truck, eh? That sounds familiar. ... You're on your way there now? How long 'til you get back here? ... A couple hours? Okay, we'll be here. ... Thanks Spike. We owe you a bunch."

He hung up his phone and announced to the kids, "They found her. Spike's going to get her right now. She'll be back in two hours."

"Oh, I'm so glad!" Violet announced.

"Yea! Mommy's coming home!" Kati shouted. Her mood completely flipped from sad to excited. "C'mon, let's go outside and play!" she suggested.

When the kids went outside to play, David pulled out his cell phone and dialed. "Hi Ted, it's David. … Well, we had a little adventure this morning. Actually, Sue did. And she's still on it. … She decided to go to Washington to talk to the Secretary. … It's okay. Spike put out an APB. The county sheriff found her in Topeka, at a Burger King by the interstate. … She got a ride in a delivery truck. Sounds familiar, doesn't it? … Deputy Leland is picking her up right now. She'll be back in two hours or so. … Okay I will. I'll call you when she gets back. Thanks Ted."

Chapter 40 – You're Back

Spike's cruiser pulled into the driveway. He and Sue got out of the car and walked around the garage to the backyard. David and the kids were waiting.

"Mommy!" Kati and Violet shouted when they saw their mother. They both ran up and hugged her tightly for several seconds.

"We're so glad you're back Mommy!" Kati told her. "We missed you. I was afraid you left for good."

"I'd never leave you two for good. I needed to go on a trip to try to fix the mess we're in. I wanted to convince people not to send us back to the base."

"You scared us," Violet told her.

"I'm sorry, Violet. I did not mean to do that to either of you," she said looking at both of her daughters. "But I'm back now. I won't leave you two again."

David came up to Sue. She stood in front of him and hung her head. "I'm sorry for leaving like that. I know it was dumb, but I had to go. I had to try to get to Washington to talk to the Secretary." She lifted her head and looked into David's eyes. "We can't all be sent back to the base. We just can't!"

"It wasn't a smart thing to do, Sue. You're back, so all is well, but don't do that again." He put his arms around her. "I'm so glad you're safe."

"I'll be going now," Spike said to David and Sue. "Call me if you need anything," he offered.

"Thank you for not making this a big deal," David said. He shook the deputy's hand. "We all really appreciate it."

"I'm just doing my civic duty," Spike replied. He turned and walked around the garage to his patrol car.

"I have to call Ted," David informed Sue. "He told me to call him when you returned."

"You called Mr. Stevens? How could you?"

"I had to. What if something happened? What if we couldn't find you? Ted had to know so he could help if we needed it."

"You didn't have to call him," she scowled. He's trying to take us back to the base. I needed to talk to the Secretary *without* Mr. Stevens."

"You know that was never going to happen. Did you think you'd make it all the way to Washington and find the Secretary and actually get a meeting with him without Ted finding out?"

"Well…"

"And did you think that the Secretary would be able to do anything about the situation?"

"I hoped."

David shook his head and chuckled. "Sue, sometimes you can be so naïve. I guess that's what I love about you. You're stubborn. You fight for what you believe in, and you think you can solve everything.

I wish I could be as steadfast and optimistic as you."

Sue smiled and hugged him.

"But I still gotta call Ted."

Sue dropped her embrace and sighed.   She knew that he had to call.

David dialed Ted's cell phone and put his phone on speaker, so Sue could hear.

"Hi David," Ted answered.   "So, what's the situation?"

"Sue is back. Say 'Hello,' Sue," David told her.

"Hi," Sue said flatly, annoyed that she had to talk to Ted.

"What were you thinking, Sue?" Ted scolded. "What did you hope to accomplish?"

"I need to talk to the Secretary. I need to tell him that all of the letters were my fault and not to blame the others."

"So you decided to stow away on a delivery truck and hitchhike all the way to Washington, D.C? Did you actually think you'd make it?"

"I made it to Kansas from California, didn't I?"

Detecting her defiance, Ted growled, and then responded, "Stay in Enterprise. Do not leave the city. Go to work and come home. And stay at your house. David, I'm counting on you to make sure she doesn't go anywhere. Escort her to work and keep her at home for one week. That's it. Just one week. And then I'll pick you up."

"What are you going to do with us, Mr. Stevens? Where are we going?" Sue demanded.

"I already told you that I will not tell you anything more. You'll find out in a week. Now stay in Enterprise and don't do anything stupid!"

"But--"

"Sue, please be good. Please. I'll see you in a week." Ted hung up his phone.

Chapter 41 - Travel Day

As they were instructed, the travelers met at David's house in the early morning to ride to the plane. Susan, Karen, and Petunia walked across the street, each wearing sun dresses. Kati and Violet also wore dresses. Zachary and Tyler wore shorts and polo shirts. David wore a buttoned dress shirt--one of the few he owned--and khaki dress pants. Sue, too, wore a sun dress. She and the others were going to look good, even if they were all being sent back to the base. They were too proud to compromise their appearance for Mr. Stevens.

As they stood outside, waiting for their ride to the airport, Susan nervously asked David, "What do Petunia and I do about our houses? Are we coming back?"

"We're coming back," David replied.

"I hope you're right," Susan countered.

A long white van arrived and pulled into the driveway. David and Sue helped the kids get in the van. The adults took seats and the van departed for Abilene.

When they arrived at the air field, the van pulled directly onto the tarmac. Ted was waiting by the stairs of the large private jet, dressed in his black suit and black tie.

"Good morning," he said with a smile.

The responses from the others were less than cordial as they boarded the plane.

Mary, Janet, and Larry were already on the plane. Mary was wearing dress slacks and a floral top. Janet wore a dress, and Larry wore a suit.

Sue and the others from Kansas hugged and shook hands in silence with the three from Wisconsin. No conversation was needed. They all had two weeks to discuss the options. They'd find out soon enough where they were going.

The co-pilot folded the stairs and locked the door. He reminded all to put on their seat belts before taking his seat in the cockpit.

The plane had barely started to move before Sue blurted out, "Where are we going, Mr. Stevens?"

"California. That's all I will tell you until we're all together. Please, Sue, sit back and relax. Enjoy the flight."

But she couldn't relax. "You're taking us back to the base, aren't you?" she lashed out. "Admit it!" she yelled in frustration.

"Back to the base?" he asked, laughing. "Is that what you think?" He laughed again, breaking the tension in the plane. "No, I'm taking you some place different. I can't tell you where just yet. You'll have to wait until the others join us. But you're not going back to the base. Trust me."

"*Can* I trust you?" Sue asked, glaring at Ted.

"Can I trust *you*?" he replied with a smile.

Sue sat back in her chair and folded her arms. The scowl didn't leave her face. She still didn't trust Ted.

The stop in Arizona was brief. It lasted only as long as it took to load Martha, Patsy and Richard, and taxi back to the runway.

Martha wore a sun dress as did Patsy. Richard wore khakis and a button-up shirt. They, too, decided that they should wear good clothes for the trip.

Within an hour, the plane landed in California and taxied to a small private hangar. When it came to a stop, the co-pilot unfolded the stairs. Ted informed the travelers that two vans were waiting to take them to their destination."

"Where are we?" Sue asked.

"Burbank, California. And the others are waiting for you in the hangar."

Ted could hardly get out of the way before the stampede of travelers exited the plane in the morning sun to greet Denise, Donald, Brandy, and Juliana. The women crowded around Denise and looked at her belly, the kids went to talk with Brandy, and the men greeted Donald.

When he joined the rest of the crowd, Ted called for quiet and attention. "We have a little trip to take in the vans. I'd like for you to split up into the two vans."

"Where are we going, Mr. Stevens?" Sue demanded. "You said you'd tell us when we met up with the others."

They all looked at Ted, waiting for an answer.

"We're not going back to the base. We're going to visit a couple people. Wait and see. You'll be pleasantly surprised."

That didn't satisfy Sue. "Why couldn't you tell us that two weeks ago?"

"Arrangements were being made. If I told you anything, you would have talked and emailed and communicated. We had to keep things quiet."

"Why?" Sue snapped.

"Security." His blunt response quieted the questions. He turned, walked to the vans and called out over his shoulder, "Now, shall we go? We're on a tight schedule."

The travelers broke into two groups and silently loaded into the vans.

The vehicles left the airport but did not get onto the freeway to reach their destination. They drove down Hollywood Way and zig-zagged through residential streets. Within ten minutes, they pulled to a stop at a school.

There were no cars in the parking lot. The only vehicles in the lot were four large black SUVs with ultra-tinted windows, idling next to the school entrance. Parked in between two of the SUVs was a black armored limo with American flags mounted on the hood by the headlights.

Ted showed his ID to the Secret Service agents blocking the driveway. They waived the vans into the lot. When the vans parked, the travelers got out and assembled together.

"Why are we here?" Donald asked.

"And where is here?" Pasty asked.

"And why is the President here?" David asked.

"We're at Theodore Roosevelt Elementary School. We're here to listen to a couple speeches. And it's not the President," Ted replied with a smile. "It's the First Lady."

Chapter 42 - VIPs

Ted escorted the group into the school. Secret Service guided Ted and his entourage to the back of the assembly room. They lined up against the back wall to listen. The school's students were already assembled toward the front. A line of media cameras and reporters stood in between the travelers and the students.

The principal of the school took the podium, greeted all those assembled and asked for quiet. She talked to the students and explained that they were very honored to have two people come and speak just to them. When she had built enough excitement, she introduced the first speaker: The Secretary of the Interior.

A tall, middle-aged man in a navy blue suit and light blue tie took the podium. He smiled at the students and greeted them warmly.

Being properly trained by their principal, they replied in unison with "Good morning Mr. Secretary."

"I'm here today to introduce a very special

person who will tell you about a new program that is being introduced all across the country. I think you'll really like it." He paused to let excitement build among the students.

"But first, I'd like to thank some very important people who helped me and the First Lady with this program. I received several letters from a concerned group of people who had a very important message. Their letters were so convincing that I went to talk with the First Lady about the idea. And that idea is why we are here today. Those very important people are standing right here in this assembly room today." He pointed to the back of the room and to the people standing against the back wall.

The children all turned around and looked at who was standing there.

More importantly, the media cameras all turned around to take pictures and video of the people standing there.

Ted stood stoically. Sue smiled and gave a little wave to the children and the cameras. The others nervously smiled, but were too embarrassed to wave.

"So now," continued the Secretary, drawing attention back up front, "without further delay, I'd like to call the First Lady of the United States to the podium to roll out this exciting new program."

He gestured to his right and the First Lady came from behind the curtains to take the podium. The students clapped loudly while the cameras flashed and clicked rapidly.

"Good morning everyone!"

"Good morning Mrs. President!" the students replied.

"It's so nice to be here with you all in Burbank,

California. What a beautiful day it is. The sky is so blue here in California. You are so lucky."

The students rustled, looking at each other. Some nodded in agreement and a few bold students even responded, "Yeah."

"I'm so excited to talk with you all today. I have some great things to tell you and to ask of you. But first…" she paused to gather maximum attention, "How many of you have a dirty bedroom?"

Several hands shot into the air and many students happily replied, "Me!"

"I thought so. Now, what happens when it gets too dirty? You have to clean it up, right?"

The students nodded in agreement.

"And who makes you clean it up? Does your mother or father ask you to clean it up?"

More nodding.

"And do they say something like 'How can you live in this room when it's so dirty?' Have you heard your parents say that before?"

Several students replied with "Yeah!" One boy close to the front boldly said "My mommy told me that this morning."

The First Lady laughed and smiled at the student. "So your mom says 'You live in this house. Clean up your room.' And you do, because you can't live in a room that keeps getting dirtier, right?"

"Yeah!"

She scanned across the study body, across the row of media and then back to the students. "Well, it's the same with Planet Earth. Our planet is dirty. Our atmosphere is dirty. Our water supply is dirty. Our oceans are heating up and so is the air temperature. There are lots of things happening to our dirty planet.

And we need to fix the damage and keep it from getting dirtier. So that's why I'm here today. I'm announcing a new program that is sponsored by me and the Secretary of the Interior. It's a program that we're taking to schools all over the country. We need the help of all students in the United States." To build attention and anticipation, she looked at the students in the front, catching some with eye-to-eye contact. "We need your help. Are you with me?"

"Yeah!" the students cheered again.

"Today we announce a new program in which we are asking school children of all ages across the country to help clean up this planet. We know that you all care about the planet and will do what is right. We need you to stop littering, keep recycling, and stop wasting electricity. And we need your help to tell your parents and other adults to do the same. So just like what your parents tell you about your bedrooms, you can tell your parents the same about the environment. You can tell them 'Hey Mom!' or 'Hey Dad! You need to clean up after yourself.' You can tell them…"

She turned to face the side wall and, on cue, two teachers held up a big banner.

The First Lady announced the new program to the students and the media, "You live on this planet. Clean up after yourself!"

Following their principal's lead, the students broke into applause. The kids all practiced the new slogan with each other as if they had just run home to tell their parents. The faculty all chatted and nodded in agreement. The media cameras panned the room to capture the event. The principal shook hands with the Secretary and First Lady.

Sue, Patsy, and Brandy ran to each other in the

back of the room and hugged in celebration. The others quickly huddled around them, hugging, shaking hands and congratulating one another. The children high-fived each other and jumped up and down with excitement. Even Ted was dragged into the mix for congratulations. Donald and David shook Ted's hand and Sue gave him the biggest hug she ever had.

Over the excitement in the room, the principal's voice became audible. "Can we please settle down?"

She waited for the noise to subside. "Thank you," she said to her students. "I want to thank our guests for launching their new program right here at Theodore Roosevelt Elementary and I hope that all of you will do your best to get your parents and friends to help you clean up after yourselves. Now, what do we have to say to our two very special guests?"

In unison, the student body responded "Thank you Mr. Secretary! Thank you Mrs. President!"

The Secretary and First Lady waved to the students and then were escorted out of the assembly room by Secret Service.

Faculty members walked into the crowd to try to corral the students back into their classrooms.

Reporters and cameramen began to pack up their equipment and move out of the assembly room to go to their vehicles parked on the streets around the school.

Brandy and the other children began to move to the door to leave.

"Hold on kids," Ted told them. "We're not leaving just yet. I've got a little surprise for all of you. If you don't mind waiting for a few minutes, I think you'll be pleased."

The last of the students exited the assembly

room in one direction and the last of the media left in the other.

After Ted and his VIPs stood alone in the assembly room for a couple minutes, Secret Service opened the door and an agent escorted the First Lady and the Secretary over to the group.

"Hi Ted," the Secretary greeted him. "Nice show, huh?"

"Well done," Ted replied. He looked at the First Lady and said, "Very well done, indeed. I think you got exactly the reception you wanted."

"You mean that *we* wanted," she replied. "This whole program was your idea, Ted."

Sue and the others stood in shock and surprise.

"No," Ted corrected the First Lady. "This whole program was not my idea. It was the idea of all of these great people here," he informed her, motioning to the nineteen people standing with him.

"May I introduce them to you?"

"Please do," she replied.

"This is Suzanne Cook," he said, guiding Sue by the arm to meet the First Lady. "She's the ring leader of this crazy circus."

"I'm very pleased to meet you, Suzanne."

"Please, call me Sue. It's a pleasure to meet you Mrs. President."

"Is this the letter writer, Ted?" the Secretary asked, referring to Sue.

"She's the one," Ted answered.

"Well, Sue, I'm honored to finally meet you. I've received so much mail from you that I wanted to meet you in person." He reached into his portfolio and pulled out all of the letters that she had sent. He handed them to Sue.

"You read them?" she asked in disbelief.

"Absolutely. I read every one of them. Well, after they were translated, I read them. Ted gave them to me. I have to say they were very convincing. I'm sorry that you got into trouble over this."

Sue looked to the Secretary and then turned to Ted. She didn't know how to say what she wanted. "It was you... You..."

Ted knew what she wanted to say. He replied, "Yes, it was me."

"I didn't know what to think of these strange letters that I received," the Secretary continued. "The FBI took them and basically closed the door on the whole thing. They told me not to concern myself with them. But then Ted came to visit me a few weeks ago. He and I go way back. He gave me the translated letters and said that he supported you. He thought that your idea was really good. He asked what I thought of a national campaign and getting the First Lady on board."

"I couldn't say no," the First Lady responded.

Sue and the others stood in awe. *Our messages have been read. And we're not in trouble at all. In fact, we're VIPs! And today we're standing with the First Lady of the United States!*

"You are a very special person," the First Lady said to Sue.

"It's not just me," Sue quickly replied. "It wasn't just me. Brandy and Patsy and Janet wrote the letters too." She pointed to the others as she rapidly talked. "And Patsy! She came up with the slogan, the one on the wall there. That was her idea. And my children helped me write the letters in our language. And Donald and Juliana and Denise and Martha and

Richard and Larry and Mary and Petunia and Susan and Karen all helped too. It was all of us!"

"Aren't you forgetting someone?" a voice came from behind her.

"Oh David!" She wheeled around and gave him a huge kiss. "I'm so sorry." She turned to the First Lady and introduced him. "This is David Hudson. He's my boyfriend and father of Zachary and Tyler. He's the reason I'm so happy in life. I don't know what I'd do without him."

"It's nice to meet you, David," the First Lady told him with a smile. "I hope you can live up to Sue's expectations,"

"I'll try," David replied. He reached his hand out and shook the First Lady's hand. "It's an honor to meet you."

The rest of the group took turns meeting the Secretary and the First Lady. The two dignitaries took the time to engage each person in conversation.

After nearly an hour, the Secret Service agent discretely informed the First Lady that it was time to leave. She and the Secretary shook hands with all one last time before leaving.

After the two departed with the Secret Service, Ted interrupted the various conversations and asked, "Who wants lunch?"

Chapter 43– To Us

It took several minutes to break up the conversations in the assembly room in order to herd the group out to the vans. Once all were on board, the two vehicles left the school. They drove for a few minutes back through the streets of Burbank, ending the ride at the airport hangar.

When everyone got out of the vans, they saw a large dining table had been laid out and set. A serving table was off to the side, full of food.

"I'm sorry I couldn't take you all some place more swanky than an airport hangar," Ted apologized sincerely. "But most places can't accommodate twenty people for lunch without prior notification."

"I think this will be lovely," Sue replied.

The others agreed.

During lunch, the friends recalled the scene at the school. And they commented on how well the slogan was received by the media and the students.

"I think we can all agree," Mary told the group, "that the letters were very effective."

"And your new language certainly got the Secretary's attention," Susan added.

"And the FBI's," Donald added with a grin.

"But I think it was Sue's persistence," David chimed in, "even though it almost got us all in trouble, that was the difference in being successful." He smiled and looked at Sue.

"It most certainly was," Ted responded. "It was that last un-encrypted letter that fully caught the attention of the Secretary. Because it was written in English, he knew then what the other letters were about. So it was easy to convince him when I gave him all of the translated letters." He smiled at Sue. "And the fact that the FBI and Homeland Security reacted so strongly to the last letter made him all the more willing to help. He doesn't trust them. If they're against something, he's usually for it." He scanned the table and smiled at everyone. "All of your work paid off. I'm proud of you all and honored to be part of your lives."

The women around the table all said "Aw," while the men raised their glasses as a toast to Ted.

"But you made it happen in the government," Sue noted.

"Then I guess we're all a great team," Ted said with a smile.

"Here here!" David called out. "To us!"

"To us!" everyone replied.

The conversation paused while everyone continued eating. After a moment, Ted broke the silence, changing the subject. "Now, Denise, what are we going to do when the baby is born?"

"What do you mean?" Denise replied.

"How are we going to celebrate?" Ted clarified.

"I don't know. I haven't given it much thought, to be honest," Denise admitted.

"Well, think about it and let us know. We're all interested in being part of your baby's life." He turned to the rest of the group and asked, "Aren't we?"

Everyone agreed.

"It will be very interesting to watch that baby grow up," Ted continued.

"In what way?" Donald asked.

"Remember back in June when I said that the children of the transformed mice in the lab had the traits of their transformed parents?" Ted asked. The others nodded in agreement, some only vaguely remembering. "Well, we can assume the same will apply to you. And the lab also discovered a few more things…" He paused to catch everyone's attention. "The transformed mice can purify pollutants better than normal mice. And the cloned mice can better control their body temperature in extreme hot or cold weather. So it seems that you eleven clones have evolutionary advantages for a changing environment that the rest of us humans don't have."

The clones all looked at each other, hearing they had another special common bond.

"Now we're about to have a child born, the child of a clone," Ted said, looking at Donald. "If that baby has the same traits as its father, then the population of evolved humans will have increased by one."

"And that means?" Sue asked.

"That means," Patsy said, "the more children, grandchildren, and future generations we have, the more people there will be with the evolved traits."

"Exactly," Ted replied. "You eleven clones will

be increasing the population of people who can better control body temperature, filter pollutants, maintain body weight; all things necessary to survive in a changing environment. And you'll be doing it by having children."

Although the full magnitude of the impact they might have was not apparent to all the clones, they at least knew they would be part of the future of Earth.

Ted continued, "By having children, and then your children having children, and so on, the evolved traits will be passed on. After many generations, there could be thousands of your descendents that have the attributes needed to thrive in a warming environment, an increasingly polluted atmosphere, an eroding ozone layer, and dwindling food supply. Your descendents may be the key to survival for humans on this planet."

Everyone sat at the table in silence, having stopped eating. They all thought about the future and the potential of the clones and their progeny.

After several minutes of thought, Sue spoke up. "Well, Ted, last year you and I sat on a plane and concluded that we clones would not take over the planet. I guess we were wrong. Eleven people *can* change the lives of three hundred million."

"Maybe even six billion," Ted replied with a smile.

Chapter 44 – See You Soon

"I'm afraid it is time to load up and head on out," Ted announced to the group.

"Do we have to leave now?" Sue asked.

"You've been talking for three hours!" We're running tight on the schedule as it is."

The others frowned, realizing it was time to leave each other, again.

"But don't feel bad," Ted added.

Nineteen faces of confusion and irritation looked at him. *Why shouldn't we feel bad?*

"We'll all be back here in Burbank in a month or two. Maybe even sooner," he said with a wink to Denise.

"That's right! The baby!" Kati called out.

"You mean we can all come back here when the baby is born?" Sue asked, not entirely believing Ted.

"Do you think I could keep you all in your houses when the next new person arrives on this planet?"

"No, probably not," Sue honestly replied.

"So I'll pick you all up and we'll fly here when Denise and Donald are ready to receive us. How's that sound?"

"Great!" Sue replied. The others agreed.

"Good. Now, can we get going? We have to take off for Phoenix," Ted informed them.

Sue started the goodbyes. She hugged Denise and told her, "I hope everything with you and your baby will be good. Only a month to go! Call us whenever you want. And Donald better call us when it's time."

"He will, I promise," Denise replied. "We'll stay in touch and we'll see you when the baby is born."

Sue next hugged Donald and told him to take good care of Denise.

"I definitely will, Sue. I've never been so happy and excited than I am now," he said.

"And you, Brandy," Sue began as she walked over to Brandy, "you are my partner in writing. None of what we saw today could have been possible without you. I think we did pretty good, don't you?"

"I do," Brandy replied. "We make a pretty good team. And Patsy too."

"Now all we have to do is keep the campaign going," Sue added. "You live on this planet…"

"Clean up after yourself!" Brandy laughed along with Sue.

"Take care of your mother and Donald, okay?" Sue said. "And keep sending emails and calling. We want to know all that's happening, okay?"

"I will," Brandy said. She gave Sue a big hug.

Sue finally hugged Juliana and said, "Please keep a close eye on Denise, will you? And stay in touch. We'll see you soon."

"I will, Sue. Thanks. And you keep an eye on those kids, alright? And keep an eye on David too," she added with a smile and a wink.

The others followed Sue and said goodbye to Denise, Donald, Brandy, and Juliana, each specially wishing good health to Denise and good luck with the baby.

Even Ted joined the others to say goodbye. When he finished, he called out above the whine of the jet engines, "Okay folks! Time to go! Everyone please get on board!"

The travelers walked up the steps of the plane and took their seats. Those with window seats waved to those staying in Burbank. The co-pilot folded the stairs, locked the door, and took his seat in the cockpit.

The plane taxied to the runway and took off.

An hour later, the plane circled and landed in Phoenix. Ted informed the others they couldn't afford fifteen minutes of goodbyes. He asked if all could stay on board and bid farewell to Martha, Patsy, and Richard from the plane.

Sue hugged Richard and asked him to take care of Patsy. He promised he would. She hugged Patsy and said, "We did a good job with our letters, don't you think?"

"Definitely. Brandy and Janet get the credit too. And so do the kids for actually writing the letters."

"I liked seeing your slogan up on the banner today. You really are smart and really creative."

Patsy blushed and responded, "Thanks."

"Keep in touch and we'll see you soon." Sue smiled.

"I look forward to it. Goodbye, Sue."

Sue next hugged Martha and told her, "It was

great to see you again, as always."

"It was," Martha agreed. "And we'll see each other soon."

"I'm so glad you like your new life. And you're really good at it. Keep me updated on Patsy and Richard," she said with a sly smile. "I want to know if wedding bells will be ringing soon."

"Ooh, you're such a gossip!" Martha teased her with a smile. "I'll send you updates. And you have to tell me about you and David." She leaned in close and said, "The others think wedding bells may also be ringing soon for you."

Sue responded with a sly smile, "We'll see."

Ted hurried the goodbyes along, reminding everyone that they'd see each other soon. Richard, Patsy, and Martha finally exited the plane and got in the car waiting to take them home.

The co-pilot closed the door and returned to his seat. Sue waved out her window as the plane started to taxi to the runway.

Chapter 45 – Happy Birthday

When the van dropped off the Kansas travelers in David's driveway, they decided to have a late dinner together. David fired up the grill. Petunia and Susan went to their houses to find side dishes for the meal. Sue instructed the children go change into play clothes. She accompanied her daughters to their house so she could change too.

After twenty minutes, much longer than was usually needed to change her clothes, Sue joined the adults at the table on the patio, carrying an envelope. She sat down next to David and told him to read the letter inside. When he finished reading, he looked at her very confused.

"And there's a building permit stuck to the front door," Sue told him.

"Really?" he asked.

Sue nodded.

"What's up?" Susan asked. "What's the letter say?"

"Ted has arranged for an addition to my

house," Sue replied. "He's paid for adding a garage and three new rooms upstairs over the porch."

"He did? Why would he do that?" Petunia inquired.

"Because Sue asked him," David responded.

When Susan and Petunia looked at him with confusion, he clarified, "In June, Sue and I talked about sharing a house so we could spend more time together. That way, the boys and girls could all have their own rooms in the same house with us." He laughed as he continued, "Sue was bold enough to actually ask Ted to pay for it."

"She has no fear," Susan noted with a smile.

"And of course, Ted can't say no to Sue," David added.

"Well, I guess congratulations are in order," Petunia said.

"It's my birthday present," Sue told them.

"Has it been a year already?" Susan asked.

"Almost," Sue replied. "Next Monday."

"We'll have to celebrate," Susan told her.

"I think we should," Sue agreed with a smile.

The kids filtered back to David's patio where the adults were sitting, and David started dinner.

The children were less active than usual. Traveling to California and back, along with the excitement of meeting the First Lady and seeing their slogan on the big banner, tapped a lot of their energy.

When dinner was served, the group dined in relative quiet; a rare, practically never-seen event with the five kids. They remembered the events of the day and congratulated each other for the success of the letter-writing campaign.

As the sun set and they sat around the table,

Kati's and Karen's eyelids became heavy. Susan and Petunia said goodnight and guided Karen home. David helped the boys into the house to change and go to sleep. Sue and Violet helped Kati walk to their house. Sue helped the girls get changed into their pajamas.

After the kids were tucked in bed, Sue and David met in the middle of the yard. The lights from David's patio dimly lit the grass where they stood. She put her arm around him and he put his arm around her. They silently stared at Sue's house.

Finally, Sue said, "I wonder what it's like to be pregnant."

About the Author

Andrew D. Carlson is a scientist and a writer. He received a Bachelor of Arts degree in chemistry from St. Olaf College. Andrew has worked in the biotech/pharmaceutical industry for over twenty-five years.

Andrew also wrote the first novel in this series; *Sue's Fingerprint*, which is available at Amazon.

Andrew lives in Los Angeles with his wife and son.

Follow Andrew at http://andrewdcarlson.com
on Twitter: @andrewdcarlson
on Facebook: Sue's Fingerprint